第三版
Third Edition

教育部推荐使用大学外语类教材
全国高等学校第二届优秀教材特等奖
国家教委高等学校第二届优秀教材一等奖

国优教材

# 大学英语 听说

# College English

总主编 董亚芬

## FOCUS LISTENING AND SPEAKING

教师用书 TEACHER'S BOOK

## Book 6


主 编 虞苏美 李慧琴
编 者 (以姓氏笔画为序)
关肇远 李慧琴 吴稚倩
邹瑶美 虞苏美




上海外语教育出版社
外教社 SHANGHAI FOREIGN LANGUAGE EDUCATION PRESS

图书在版编目(CIP)数据

听说. 第6册 / 虞苏美，李慧琴主编；关肇远等编. 3版.
—上海：上海外语教育出版社，2008
大学英语(第三版) / 董亚芬总主编
教师用书
ISBN 978-7-5446-0710-0

I. 听… II. ①虞… ②李… ③关… III. 英语—听说教学—高等学校—教学参考资料
IV. H319.9

中国版本图书馆CIP数据核字(2008)第028804号

出版发行：上海外语教育出版社
(上海外国语大学内) 邮编：200083
电 话：021-65425300(总机)
电子邮箱：bookinfo@sflep.com.cn
网 址：http://www.sflep.com.cn http://www.sflep.com
责任编辑：曹 娟

印 刷：江苏句容排印厂
经 销：新华书店上海发行所
开 本：787×1092 1/16 印张11.5 字数242千字
版 次：2008年8月第1版 2008年8月第1次印刷
印 数：5 000册

书 号：ISBN 978-7-5446-0710-0 / H·0319
定 价：19.00元

# 《大学英语》第三版 编委会名单

# 总序

《大学英语》是遵照1986年国家教委审定的《大学英语教学大纲（文理科本科用）》编写的一套系列教材，分精读、泛读、听说、快速阅读和语法与练习五种教程，由全国六所重点大学合作编写。教材于1986年出版试用本，1992年出版正式本，并于同年9月荣获全国高等学校第二届优秀教材特等奖，以及国家教委高等学校第二届优秀教材一等奖。

1998年，在广泛征求意见的基础上，《大学英语》系列教材根据《大学英语教学大纲（高等学校本科用）》进行了第一次修订。修订本更加注意文、理、工、农、医等各科的通用性，力求给学生打好“宽、厚、牢”的语言基础。

为了推进大学英语教学改革，适应社会各界对大学生英语能力的要求，教育部于2004年颁布了《大学英语课程教学要求（试行）》（以下简称《课程要求》）。遵照《课程要求》对大学英语提出的教学目标，即“培养学生的英语综合应用能力”，编者于2004年决定对教材进行第二次修订，以满足新时期国家和社会对人才培养的需要。

**本次修订原则：**

1. 教材的定位不变。《大学英语》是综合教育型（English for integrative purposes）而非特殊目的型（English for specific purposes）的教材，旨在帮助大学本科各专业学生进一步打下扎实的语言基础。

2. 选材原则不变。正因为《大学英语》是综合教育型的，选材必须做到题材广泛，体裁多样，语言规范，有利于打好语言基础。选材遵循三性原则，即趣味性、知识性、可思性，以激发学生学习英语的兴趣。

3. 在更新课文时注意经典性与时代性的融合，科普性与文学性的融合，使选文内容经得起时间考验，文字经得起反复咀嚼。这两个融合是教材可教性与可学性的保证，也是教材生命力之所在。

4. 本次修订按照《课程要求》所提出的培养“英语综合应用能力”这一目标，着重考虑增强听与说的训练，提高听与说尤其是说的要求。

**本次修订重点：**

**精读：**

1. 更新部分课文。选用一些时代感更强、更贴近现代生活、语言更地道的文章取代部分相形见绌的课文。

2. 梳理全教程的练习。除了设置新的听、说练习外，还针对近年来学生在口、笔试中经常出现的语言错误设计了用法方面的练习，以提高学生在使用英语时的准确性。

3. 为了帮助学生集中精力学好基本词语，这次修订继续遵循前次修订时的方法，把全书单词分为三类：（1）words to drill（通过反复操练能熟练掌握其用法的单词）；（2）words to remember（能记住其形、音、义的单词）；（3）words to have a nodding acquaintance with（能于再次出现时根据上下文识别其词义的单词），并进一步调整各项练习，以确保常用词语的复现率。

4. 为了提高学生的写作能力，这次修订还强调微观与宏观的写作技能同时发展，即一方面训练学生如何写好各类句子，同时从第一课开始就要求学生写成段的文章。

**泛读：**

在第一次修订的基础上进一步选用时代感较强、故事情节动人的文章取代内容相对陈旧的课文。丰富了练习类型（如增加了词汇练习和翻译练习），以帮助学生在提高阅读理解能力的同时适当扩大词汇量。

**听说：**

除了大幅度更新听力材料，适当提高听力理解的要求之外，这次修订还有针对性地增强了说的训练。根据不同话题提供了丰富的口语素材，并通过多种练习方式为培养学生具有实质性的口语能力打下基础。

**快速阅读：**

除了原有的版本继续发行之外，还另外编写了一套全新的快速阅读教程，内容侧重科普，供各类院校选择使用。

**语法与练习：**

把原有四册书删繁就简为两册，以便于学生携带。删除部分章节，增补和替换了大量例句和练习。为方便学生自学，例句都附有中文译文。本教程既可作为语法参考书，也可作为补充练习手册。

**精读（预备级）、泛读（预备级）、听说（预备级）：**

分别将精读(预备级)和泛读(预备级)由原来的各两册修订成各一册。精读(预备级)为重新设计编写，不仅课文与练习是全新的，对听与说的要求也比原书有较明显的提高。泛读(预备级)和听说(预备级)也作了相应的更新与改进。

本教材的起点为1 800单词，从这个起点开始要为学生打下扎实的语言基础并达到培养英语综合应用能力这一目标，教材除了必须提供丰富的语言素材之外，还必须编写出多种口笔头练习以保证学生有足够的语言实践机会。因此本教材的精、泛读教程仍坚持每册编写10单元。但目前大学英语的有效授课时间有限，各校可以根据学生的具体情况制定自己的教学计划，灵活选用练习，不必每题必做。与此同时还应当尽可能争取合理的周学时并充分调动学生课外自学的积极性。如果师生双方能共同努力，相互配合，认真学好每一单元，则必能取得良好的教学效果。

《大学英语》从试用本问世到本次修订本完稿历时20余载，跨越两个世纪。使用者一度遍及全国千余所高等院校，受到了师生们的广泛欢迎。教材之所以有这样的规模和影响力主要可以归结为以下几个原因：

（1）一支优秀的编写队伍：《大学英语》的编者为来自全国六所重点大学的骨干教师，他们都有长期的大学英语教学经历，具备深厚的英、汉语功底与高度负责的工作态度。这是本套教材获得大学英语教学界普遍认同的基础。

（2）精心挑选的精、泛读课文和听力材料：课文为教材之本，能否为读者提供理想的课文是教材成功的关键。不少人认为当前选材自由度很大，各类原版的素材铺天盖地，俯拾即是，选材不存在困难。然而事实证明，选材却是编写工作中最为辛苦费力的环节。《大学英语》的编者们虽然长期积累了大量素材，但为了找出更合适的内容，往往需要翻阅数十篇甚至上百篇文章才能筛选出一段文字优美纯正，内容引人入胜的选文材料，正是这样，才确保了课文的趣味性、知识性和可思性。

（3）科学设计和认真编写的练习：在编写和历次修订的过程中，本书编者不仅重视练习的针对性和实用性，还十分注重练习的语言质量。几乎每个例句都经过了集体讨论、反复推敲和论证，以确保语言规范、内容完整和难易度适中，使学生能够在轻轻松松的课堂气氛中进行语言操练。

（4）审稿层层把关：为了使教材更完善，在正式定稿前，约请了多位中外专家多次审阅和润饰。

除了上述各点外，本教材经久不衰的另一重要原因是广大读者多年来的支持和关爱。他们通过文章、书信和座谈等渠道，在充分肯定我们教材的同时，还向我们提出了不少宝贵的意见和建议，对我们的再修订工作助益颇丰。对此，我代表编写组全体成员向他们表示最诚挚的感谢，并衷心希望他们能够一如既往地支持我们的教材，随时向我们反馈各种意见和建议。

《大学英语》系列教材（第三版）由复旦大学、北京大学、华东师范大学、南京大学、四川大学、苏州大学等高校的资深教授、英语教学专家通力合作，修订编写而成。英籍专家Anthony Ward协助编写与审阅。出版社的同志协助编写组安排修订日程，随时提出改进的意见和建议，协调有关编写和编辑工作，为保证这次修订工作的顺利完成付出了辛勤的劳动。在此一并致以诚挚的感谢。

总主编　董亚芬

2006年3月

# 编者的话

本书为《大学英语》系列教材(第三版)听说教程(Focus Listening and Speaking)。现就本次修订的构思作如下说明:

## 修订的基本原则

鉴于目前大学生的英语听力水平有普遍的、大幅度的提高，同时教育部颁布的《大学英语课程教学要求(试行)》(以下简称《课程要求》)又把听说的要求提高了一个层次，我们于2004年5月开始对本教程进行再次修订，以适应新时代形势发展的需要。第三版在原有基础上有一定的创新和突破，以更有助于进一步提高学生的听说能力。

根据《课程要求》和当前学生的英语听说水平，本教程第五册至第六册的再修订工作围绕以下几个方面进行:

1. 宗旨
   1) 帮助学生掌握必要的听力技能;
   2) 进一步提高学生在语篇水平上的听力理解能力;
   3) 帮助学生掌握多种交际功能，培养学生口头表达的能力;
   4) 逐步培养学生单句和成段说话的能力。
2. 话题　保留原来五至六册80%的话题，另外20%则为新增贴近时代的话题。
3. 选文　力求课文语言流畅、地道和规范；内容具有趣味性和时代气息。保留60%使用效果较好的篇目，其余40%左右的课文均为新选材料。
4. 说的训练　组织学生围绕课文内容进行对话及讨论，提供表达各种交际功能的日常口语以及样板对话，设置情景，多方为学生提供口语活动的机会，以提高他们的实质性的口语能力(即能言之有物)。
5. 录音语速　以保证达到《课程要求》对学生提出的听力要求，教程的选文以正常语速录音。

## 编写框架

本书为听说教程第六册的教师用书。全书共十个单元，设十个话题。十个单元后提供两套综合试题。

每单元设A、B、C、D、E五个部分:

**Part A　Listening Activities　听力训练**

这部分提供两个练习，旨在帮助学生1) 获取重要的交际能力，2) 掌握多种听力技能。

**Part B　Speaking Activities　口语训练**

这部分的口语活动主要围绕课文内容及各种交际功能展开。练习形式由浅入深，有利于启发学生开口。每逢双课提供与课文话题有关的交际功能及常用语言表达方式，通过练习使学生学到如何得体地进行日常对话。

**Part C　Listen and Relax　听力欣赏**

这部分的内容有歌曲、诗歌、幽默、笑话、谜语、绕口令、谚语、名人名言等，旨在让学生在三至五分钟轻松的语言环境中培养语感, 提高学习兴趣。

**Part D　Further Listening　听力提高训练**

形式为与课文同一话题的两篇听力材料和练习。练习题的形式多种多样，旨在提高学生的理解能力和应变能力。

**Part E　Home Listening　课外听力训练**

提供两篇与课文同一话题的听力材料及练习，供学生课外自学。

## 使用说明

1. 每单元1.5课时。其中Part A听力训练 (Listening Activities), Part C听力欣赏部分 (Listen and Relax) 以及Part D听力提高训练 (Further Listening) 可安排在一课时内完成。

2. Part B口语训练 (Speaking Activities) 是本教程的一个重点。建议用半课时的时间完成该部分的练习。教师亦可根据学生的具体情况选择部分练习操练。

3. Part E课外听力训练 (Home Listening) 务必布置学生在课外完成。

4. 书末的两套测试题可以在课内完成, 或布置学生在课外进行自测。

本书由华东师范大学大学英语教学部负责编写。虞苏美和李慧琴任主编。参加修订的有 (以姓氏笔画为序) 关肇远、李慧琴、吴稚倩、邹瑶美和虞苏美。

在本书的修订过程中，复旦大学董亚芬教授提出了许多宝贵的意见和建议。英籍专家Anthony Ward对全书作了审阅。此外，马雨默女士为前言和附录部分做了不少工作。在教材出版之际，谨向他们表示由衷的感谢。

本书录音磁带由上海外语音像出版社出版发行。

编者

2007年11月

# Contents

## *Contents*

# Contents

# Unit 1

## An Investigation

## Part A Listening Activities

### A Conversation

## A Good Observer

| | |
|---|---|
| **Officer** | Mrs Dawson, thanks very much for coming down to the station. I ... I know you've been through a heck of a situation here today. Um ... I'd just like to go over some of the things that you told Sergeant Palmer at the bank. |
| **Mrs Dawson** | All right. |
| **Officer** | Uh, would you like a cup of coffee? |
| **Mrs Dawson** | No. No, I'm fine. (All right.) Thanks. |
| **Officer** | Well, um ... c-c-could you describe the two people who robbed the bank for this |

report that we're filling out here? Now, anything at all that you can remember would be extremely helpful to us.

**Mrs Dawson** Well ... uh ... just ... I can only remember basically what I said before. (That's all right.) The man was tall ... uh ... six foot, six foot one, (Mm-hmm?) and he had dark hair, (Dark hair.) and he had a moustache.

**Officer** Very good. All right, did he have any other distinguishing marks, I mean scars, for example, anything like that?

**Mrs Dawson** Scars ... um ... (Mm-hmm.) no. No, none that I can remember.

**Officer** Do you remember how old he was, by any chance?

**Mrs Dawson** Uh ... well, I ... I guess around thirty, (Around thirty.) m ... maybe younger, give or take a few years.

**Officer** Mm hmm. All right, do you, uh, remember anything about what he might have been wearing?

**Mrs Dawson** Yes. Yes, he ... he had on a dark sweater, a ... (Mm-hmm.) a solid color.

**Officer** OK, um ... anything else that strikes you (Um ...) at the moment?

**Mrs Dawson** I ... I remember he was wearing a light shirt under the sweater. (Ah, very good.) Yes, yes.

**Officer** Mm-hmm. All right, now, can you tell us anything about the, uh, the woman robber, uh, Mrs Dawson?

**Mrs Dawson** Well, the biggest thing that I remember about her was that she did most of the talking. (Mm-hmm) She had the gun pointed at us and she told us to lie down on the floor (Hmm.) and not to move if we knew what was good for us. (Hmm.) I remember it just felt like she was pointing the gun right at me, and my little son was right next to me and he ... he was just so frightened ...

**Officer** Uh, Mrs Dawson, could you describe her for us?

**Mrs Dawson** Ugh. She was wearing a wool sweater ... (Ah, very good.) I remember it was a dark color, (Mm-hmm.) navy blue or ... or black, (Black, mm-hmm.) and I guess she was in her late twenties. Uh, her hair was short, (Mm-hmm.) very short and curly.

**Officer** Do you remember how tall she was?

**Mrs Dawson** Uh ... a ... about the same as myself, (Mm-hmm.) around five four.

**Officer** Five four, mm-hmm. All right, do you, uh ... remember anything else about this woman?

**Mrs Dawson** Yes. I remember that the woman was wearing a pendant or a ... or a locket around her neck. (Uh-huh.) I remember specifically because my little boy started to cry (Oh.) and the woman came up to me and said, "Shut your damn kid up, lady." (Mm-hmm.) So I got a good look at the woman and ... and she was sort of, uh, pulling on the chain, uh,

playing with it. (Oh?) It was gold, uh, well anyway, it looked like gold.

**Officer** Mm-hmm. Did either of them have any other, uh, noticeable characteristics, Mrs Dawson? Now, just take a moment to (No, I don't ...) think about this.

**Mrs Dawson** No. No, a-a and this is really all I can remember.

**Officer** Well, did either of them wear glasses?

**Mrs Dawson** No. No, I'm sure of that.

**Officer** Mm-hmm. All right, Mrs Dawson, I really appreciate what you've been through today. I'm just going to ask you to look at some photographs before you leave, if you don't mind. It won't take very long. Can you do that for me?

**Mrs Dawson** Oh, a-all right.

**Officer** Would you like to step this way with me, please?

**Mrs Dawson** OK. Sure.

**Officer** Thank you.

## *New Words and Expressions*

| | | | |
|---|---|---|---|
| sergeant | /ˈsɑːdʒənt/ | *n.* | 警察小队长 a police officer ranking immediately below a captain or a lieutenant in the U.S. and immediately below an inspector in Britain |
| moustache | /məsˈtɑːʃ/ | *n.* | 八字须 hair that grows above the upper lip |
| distinguishing | /dɪsˈtɪŋgwɪʃɪŋ/ | *adj.* | 明显的 distinctive |
| scar | /skɑː/ | *n.* | 疤痕 a mark left on the skin by a healed cut or a burn |
| curly | /ˈkɜːlɪ/ | *adj.* | 卷曲的 (of hair) having a curving shape |
| pendant | /ˈpendənt/ | *n.* | 挂件 a piece of jewelry worn around the neck consisting of a long chain with an object hanging from it |
| locket | /ˈlɒkɪt/ | *n.* | （挂在项链下用以珍藏亲人头发、照片等的）小盒 a small case for a miniature portrait or a lock of hair, usually worn on a necklace |

| | |
|---|---|
| be through | 经历 to go through |

| | | |
|---|---|---|
| a heck of a situation | | 极糟糕的景况 a hell of a situation, a very bad situation |
| fill out | | 填写 to give written information by completing a form |
| by any chance | | 有没有可能 an expression used in enquiring about the possibility of something |
| give or take a few years | | 相差不到几岁 plus or minus a few years |
| Palmer | /ˈpɑːmə(r)/ | 姓 surname |
| Dawson | /ˈdɔːsən/ | 姓 surname |

## Language and Culture Notes

***Background Information*** Robbery is a serious social problem in the West. Bank robbery, in particular, is most threatening, for in nine out of ten cases robbers tend to be armed. To solve a robbery case the police must go through a lot of investigations, for example, interviewing eyewitnesses, narrowing down the suspects and so on.

### Exercise 1

**Listen to the conversation. Then choose the right answer to each question you hear.**

1. What's the probable relationship between the two speakers?
   a. A bank manager and a customer.
   b. A police officer and a woman robber.
   c. A policeman and a bank manager.
   d. A police officer and an eyewitness to a robbery.

2. When and where does the conversation take place?
   a. At Mrs Dawson's home, on the day after the robbery.

b. Inside the bank, immediately after the robbery.

c. At the police station, on the day of the robbery.

d. At the scene of the robbery, on the day the bank was robbed.

3. Which of the following is NOT mentioned in the conversation?

a. The woman robber was armed.

b. The woman robber talked a lot.

c. The woman robber was in her late twenties.

d. Neither of the robbers wore glasses.

4. What was Mrs Dawson going to do at the end of the conversation?

a. Look at some pictures of the two robbers.

b. Look at some pictures of suspects.

c. Go to another room to have her picture taken.

d. Fill in a report.

5. What can you infer from the conversation?

a. Mrs Dawson was the only witness to the robbery.

b. Mrs Dawson worked at the bank.

c. Mrs Dawson was a customer at the bank.

d. Mrs Dawson was not brave.

## Exercise 2

**Listen to the conversation again. Then fill in the chart with the necessary information about the man and the woman robbers.**

| | Man Robber | Woman Robber |
|---|---|---|
| **Height** | six foot one | around five four |
| **Hair** | dark | very short and curly |
| **Age** | around thirty | in her late twenties |
| **Clothing** | light shirt, dark sweater | dark-colored wool sweater |

# Part B Speaking Activities

## Pair Work

### Exercise 1

**Describe the two robbers in your own words with the help of the above chart.**

*Suggested answers:*

1. The man robber was around thirty, maybe a few years younger or older. He was rather tall, about six foot one in height. He had dark hair and a moustache. There were no scars on his face. He was wearing a dark sweater under which he had on a light shirt.
2. The woman robber was in her late twenties. She was around five foot four in height. Her hair was very short and curly. She was wearing a wool sweater of a dark color, and a pendant or a locket with a gold chain around her neck.

### Exercise 2

**Listen to the conversation again and pay attention to the questions the police officer asked to elicit information from Mrs Dawson about the appearance of the two robbers. Then work in pairs and act out the following role play. Take turns to play the part of the police detective and that of the witness.**

You are a police detective. A few days ago, two burglars broke into a shop and made away with some cash and a laptop computer. You have narrowed the suspects down to two people, one man and one woman. A taxi driver came forward in answer to police inquiries. He said that he witnessed the crime. Find out from the taxi driver what the two burglars looked like and fill in the chart below.

| | Burglar 1 | Burglar 2 |
|---|---|---|
| **Male / Female** | | |
| **Height** | | |
| **Hair** | | |
| **Age** | | |
| **Clothing** | | |

# Part C Listen and Relax

## A Poem

**You're going to hear a poem written by the English poet A.E. Housman. Try to learn it by heart.**

### *When I Was One-and-Twenty*

*When I was one-and-twenty*
*I heard a wise man say,*
*"Give crowns and pounds and guineas*
*But not your heart away;*
*Give pearls away and rubies*
*But keep your fancy free."*
*But I was one-and-twenty*
*No use to talk to me.*

*When I was one-and-twenty*
*I heard him say again,*
*"The heart out of the bosom*
*was never given in vain;*
*'Tis paid with sighs a-plenty*

*And sold for endless rue."*
*And I am two-and-twenty*
*And oh, 'tis true, 'tis true.*

*— A. E. Housman*

**Notes**

1. Alfred Edward Housman (1859 — 1936): English scholar and poet. His major collections of poetry are *A Shropshire Lad* (1896), *Last Poems* (1922) and *More Poems*, published posthumously in 1936.
2. 'tis: it is
3. rue: sorrow, remorse

# Part D Further Listening

## A Story

### A Real Life Story

**Exercise**

**You are going to hear a story. Listen carefully and choose the right answer to each question you hear.**

I was having some photos developed at a photo shop in the town center one sunny Saturday morning and I was waiting outside. A nice lady approached me and asked me if I wanted to enter a competition. The first prize was a weekend trip to London for two people. She had lots of coupons with her and she took down my details — name, age, address and telephone number. I thanked her and left.

Imagine my astonishment and happiness when I found out that I had won the first prize! I was on cloud nine because I knew I didn't have the money for the holiday. The company sent us our train

tickets and the following Saturday morning my husband and I left Edinburgh for a weekend in London. We were really excited about the trip. I'd had my hair cut and my husband had had his suit dry-cleaned. Five hours later, we arrived in London and went straight to the hotel where our room had been booked by the company. That's when we got our first shock; the receptionist said there was no booking in our name. We told him about the competition prize, but he said that the hotel was unaware of anything like that. We were angry, but not suspicious. We decided to return to Edinburgh. We had our luggage put in a taxi and went back to the train station. Late on Saturday night we arrived home, tired and disappointed. Strangely, when my husband put his key in the lock, he discovered that it was already open. At that moment, it all made sense; I knew the house had been broken into and that we had been tricked. The whole house was upside down. It was a complete mess. They had taken everything, our money, jewellery, the TV, video, stereo and the microwave oven. They had even helped themselves to the food in the fridge and left a note which said: "We hope you had a nice time — we certainly did. By the way, you should have your house redecorated!"

Well, we called the police and had the house checked for fingerprints, but none were found. Clearly, our house hadn't been burgled by amateurs — they were real professionals. We're going to have an alarm installed now and we're having the locks changed too. Luckily, the house is insured so we can replace everything. But it's a horrible feeling when you find your home has been invaded like that.

1. What happened to the speaker one Saturday morning?
   a. She met a nice lady at a photo shop.
   b. She was asked to enter a competition.
   c. She was given lots of coupons.
   d. She was offered two tickets for a weekend trip to London.

2. When did the couple get their first shock?
   a. When they arrived in London.
   b. When they found that no hotel room had been booked for them.
   c. When the hotel people said they knew nothing about the competition.
   d. When the hotel people told them they knew nothing about the prize.

3. What did they decide to do then?
   a. To stay on in London for a few days.
   b. To return immediately to Edinburgh.
   c. To call the company that sent them the tickets for an explanation.
   d. To go to the police to report the matter.

4. What did they find when they returned home?
   a. Their house was dirty and messy.
   b. Some strangers had come to stay in their house.
   c. The key to their lock didn't work.
   d. All the valuable things in their house were taken away by burglars.

5. Which of the following is true of the couple?
   a. They were easily tricked.
   b. They suffered heavy losses.
   c. They were the sort of people who sought small gains but received heavy losses.
   d. They would have their house redecorated.

## A Conversation

### Solving a Crime

#### Exercise

**Listen to the conversation and write down your answers to the following questions.**

Thomas Price parked his car and went around the corner to buy a newspaper at the drugstore. His friend Linda Grant was waiting for him in the car. Suddenly she heard a shot. Then she heard another shot. She ran to the store to see what had happened. She found her friend Thomas there. He was holding a gun. The owner of the store was lying on the floor, dead. The police have just arrived on the scene and a detective is questioning Linda and Thomas. What evidence does the detective need to solve the crime?

**Detective** Tell me what happened, Miss Grant.

**Linda** I was sitting in the car waiting for Thomas. Suddenly I heard shots. I ran to the store.

**Detective** What did you see there?

**Linda** I saw Thomas standing by the dead man. Thomas was holding a gun.

**Detective** So you did see him with the gun in his hand; and you heard someone fire shots.

**Linda** Yes. But Thomas didn't kill the man.

**Detective** How do you know that he didn't?

**Linda** It's too difficult for me to explain. Why don't you ask Thomas?

**Detective** OK, Mr Price. Tell me your story.

**Thomas** I was walking toward the store when I heard a shot. I pulled out my gun and ran into the store.

**Detective** What happened next?

**Thomas** I saw the owner of the store lying on the floor and another man jumping out the window. The cash register was empty.

**Detective** Did you fire any shots?

**Thomas** Absolutely not.

**Detective** Why were you carrying a gun?

**Thomas** Because I work alone in another store and I need protection.

**Detective** How do I know that you're telling the truth?

**Thomas** It's difficult to prove.

**Linda** Thomas always tells the truth. He's completely honest.

**Detective** Actually figuring out if Thomas was innocent won't be difficult in this case. We only have to find out if the owner of the store was killed by Thomas's gun.

1. Why did Thomas go to the store?
   *To buy a newspaper.*
2. How many shots did Linda hear?
   *Two shots.*
3. What was Thomas's story?
   *He said he was walking toward the store when he heard a shot. Then he pulled out his gun and ran into the store. And he saw the owner of the store lying on the floor and another man jumping out the window. The cash register was empty.*
4. How did Linda know that Thomas didn't kill the store-owner?
   *Linda said that Thomas always told the truth and he was completely honest.*
5. Why did Thomas carry a gun?
   *He worked alone in another store and he needed protection.*
6. How can the detective prove that Thomas was innocent?
   *By finding out whether the bullet that killed the store owner was fired from Thomas's gun.*

# Part E Home Listening

## Conversation 1

# Dealing with a Crime

### Exercise

**Listen to the conversation and supply the missing information in the chart.**

**Police** Hello. Midtown South Precinct.

**Rose** Hello. I want to report a burglary.

**Police** What's your address, please?

**Rose** 415 West 44th Street, Apartment 3B.

**Police** Yes, that's our district. When did the burglary take place?

**Rose** Sometime today. I left for work at 8 a.m. and when I got home at 6 p.m., I found my apartment had been burglarized.

**Police** Does the superintendent live in the building?

**Rose** Yes, he lives downstairs on the first floor. But he says he didn't see anyone suspicious. It looks like they came in from the fire escape. The window over the fire escape is broken.

**Police** What's your name, please?

**Rose** Rose Silver.

**Police** What did you lose, Mrs Silver?

**Rose** Let's see. I have the list here. Oh, a color TV, a stereo, a laptop, two oil paintings, some jewelry and some clothes. They must have had a truck waiting downstairs.

**Police** Don't touch anything, Mrs Silver. We'll have someone out there in about ten minutes. We'll need the serial numbers of the TV, the stereo and the computer if you have them.

**Rose** OK.

| A Policeman's Report | |
|---|---|
| Name of the person who reported the crime | Rose Silver |
| Type of crime | *burglary* |
| Time of the crime | sometime between 8 a.m. to *6 p.m.* |
| Scene of the crime | *415* West *44th* Street Apt. *3B* |
| Losses | a color TV, a *stereo*, a laptop, two *oil paintings*, some *jewelry and clothes* |

## Conversation 2

# Reporting an Incident

### Exercise

**You're going to hear a conversation between a man and a police officer. Listen carefully and choose the right answer to each question you hear.**

**Man** Constable. Constable!

**Police officer** Yes, sir. What seems to be the trouble?

**Man** I'd like to report a robbery. It's my car. It's been stolen.

**Police officer** I see. And where was the vehicle parked at the time?

**Man** Just round the corner here in Water Street. I left it there about an hour ago and now it's gone!

**Police officer** Water Street, you say? Are you sure?

**Man** Of course. I'm absolutely sure.

**Police officer** And you parked it there at about ... ten o'clock?

**Man** Yes, that's right. I bet some young thug has stolen it. These young people, they have no respect for the law these days, I …

**Police officer** Yes, sir. Well, you'd better just give me a few details so that we can see about tracing the vehicle. What kind of car is it?

**Man** It's a BMW 540i.

**Police officer** Color?

**Man** It's red.

**Police officer** Red? And the registration number?

**Man** P67 HKL.

**Police officer** HKL. Right. Just a minute, sir. We've got a report here of a vehicle that has been removed from Water Street. It's a red BMW 540i. Registration number P67 HKL. Yes, that's right.

**Man** Well ...?

**Police officer** Just a moment, sir. They're checking whether anything has been reported about the vehicle.

**Man** Well, I hope it's not going to take too long. I'm a busy man. If I get my hands on the young hooligans that have taken it, I'll …

**Police officer** Excuse me, sir. You've got it.

**Man** Great! Has it already been found?

**Police officer** Not exactly.

**Man** It hasn't been damaged, has it?

**Police officer** No, sir. I don't suppose it's been damaged because it was never stolen.

**Man** What do you mean?

**Police officer** It was towed away at 10:45 this morning.

**Man** Towed away? But, but it was only parked there for an hour!

**Police officer** Yes, sir. But cars shouldn't be parked there at all. It's a very narrow street.

**Man** But, they can't just tow away my car. Then where has my car been taken to?

**Police officer** All vehicles that have been towed away are taken to the car pound in Hilton Road.

**Man** Hilton Road? That's miles away. I haven't got time to go to the other side of the town.

**Police officer** Well, sir. Perhaps you'll have to be more careful about where you park in future.

1. What do you think happened to the man's car?
   a. It was stolen. b. It was towed away.
   c. It was driven away by some young people. d. It was damaged.

2. Which of the following is true of the car?
   a. It's a BMW 540ix.
   b. It's now at the police station.
   c. It isn't damaged.
   d. It was parked in Water Street for a couple of hours.

3. What can you learn from the conversation?
   a. The man is a new driver.
   b. The man is too busy to park his car in Hilton Street.
   c. The man shouldn't have parked his car in Water Street for so long.
   d. The man has violated traffic regulations.

# Unit 2

## Sightseeing

## Part A Listening Activities

### A Monologue

# A Tour of Washington, D.C.

**Tour guide** … I hope you all enjoyed your visit to Capitol Hill. If you look back behind you, you can get an excellent look at the Capitol Building, with its beautiful dome and the Statue of Freedom on top. I forgot to mention that the design for the original building was chosen by George Washington himself back in the 1790s. That building was opened in 1800, but it was burned down by the British during the War of 1812, and it had to be completely rebuilt.

Well, to continue our tour, ladies and gentlemen, we're now traveling west on Madison Drive. Our next stop will be the Washington Monument — five hundred fifty-five feet high and dedicated to George Washington, our first president. In the meantime, if you'll look out the windows on the right, we're just passing the National Gallery, which houses an extensive collection of European and American art from the thirteenth to the twentieth centuries ... By the way, this park-like area that we're traveling along is called the Mall. It extends from the Capitol to the Washington Monument. ... Across the Mall, on the left, is the National Air and Space Museum, with exhibits on aviation history and the space age. If you have time, I highly recommend you to visit the Air and Space Museum for a fascinating look at the history of air and space travel. You'll even get a chance to see a piece of rock from the moon. ... If you look straight ahead now, folks, you'll see the Washington Monument. The monument, an obelisk that stands five hundred fifty-five feet high, was finished in 1884. We'll be stopping there shortly and those of you who wish will be able to take photographs from the observation level five hundred feet up. There's an elevator to take you there, and it's free.

All right, everyone, here we are. We'll be staying here approximately twenty minutes. For those of you who do take the elevator up to the top, if you look directly north, you'll be able to get an excellent view of our next stop, the White House — the home of all our presidents since the second president, John Adams. ... OK, remember to take all your personal belongings as you get off the bus. We'll meet back here in twenty minutes. ...

## New Words and Expressions

| | | | |
|---|---|---|---|
| Capitol | /ˈkæpɪtəl/ | *n.* | 国会大厦（美） the building in which the US Congress meets |
| dome | /dəʊm/ | *n.* | 圆屋顶 a rounded roof on a building |
| monument | /ˈmɒnjʊmənt/ | *n.* | 纪念碑 a statue, building, or other structure erected in memory of a person, event, etc. |
| house | /haʊz/ | *v.* | 收藏有 to provide storage place for, to shelter |
| aviation | /ˌeɪvɪˈeɪʃən/ | *n.* | 航空 the activity of flying aircraft, or designing, developing and producing aircraft |
| folks | /fəʊks/ | *n.* | *(pl.)* 人们 people of a particular group (here, all the tourists in the group) |

| | | | |
|---|---|---|---|
| obelisk | /ˈɒbəlɪsk/ | *n.* | 方尖碑 a tall, rectangular stone column that rises to a pointed pyramidal top |
| belongings | /bɪˈlɒŋɪŋz/ | *n.* | *(pl.)* 所有物 the things that people owns, esp. those that they can take with them |
| observation | /ˌɒbzəˈveɪʃən/ | | 观察，观望 the act of watching something attentively |
| in the meantime | | | 同时 at the same time |
| Madison Drive | /ˈmædɪsən/ | | 麦迪逊街 name of a street in Washington, D.C. |
| the Mall | /mɔːl/ | | (国会大厦与林肯纪念堂之间的)草地广场 or the National Mall, an open-area national park in downtown Washington, D.C., often used to refer to the entire area between the Lincoln Memorial and the Capitol |

## Language and Culture Notes

1. ***Background Information*** Washington, D.C. (District of Columbia, named after Columbus) is the capital of the U.S. It is not only the home of the U.S. government (since 1800), but also an important cultural center and a living historical museum with countless treasures and monuments to America's past. However, it is also a city with a very high crime rate. From the recording we will hear a tour guide giving information about Washington, D.C. to passengers on a tour bus.
2. ***the Capitol*** Name of the building that houses the United States Congress, the body of elected representatives who make the country's laws. The Capitol sits on a hill. Therefore the area is commonly referred to as Capitol Hill.
3. ***the War of 1812*** The U.S. war against Great Britain, which was declared by the Congress on June 18, 1812, and lasted more than two years. In the summer of 1814, the city of Washington was captured temporarily by the British and the Capitol was burnt down. However, the Americans also won several decisive victories during the war. For example, the victory at Fort

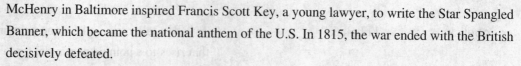

McHenry in Baltimore inspired Francis Scott Key, a young lawyer, to write the Star Spangled Banner, which became the national anthem of the U.S. In 1815, the war ended with the British decisively defeated.

4. ***the Mall*** Also called the National Mall. It is a long strip of green surrounded by museums and monuments. It stretches for over 2 miles from the Lincoln Memorial on the western border to the Capitol on the east. Along the Mall visitors can also see a number of the nation's other most popular museums, including the National Gallery of Art, the National Museum of Natural History, National Museum of American History, Washington Monument, and the National Air and Space Museum. It is the city's center of activity and a favorite place for picknickers and joggers.
5. ***the observation level*** Built at a height of 500 feet from the lobby of the Washington Monument, the place allows visitors to have a bird's-eye view of the landscape beneath.

## Exercise 1

**Listen to the recording once and choose the right answer to each question you hear.**

1. Where will the passengers stop for 20 minutes?

   a. The White House. b. Capitol Hill.

   c. The Washington Monument. d. The Mall.

2. When was the Capitol Building opened?

   a. In 1812. b. In 1800.

   c. In 1790. d. In 1884.

3. What are the tourists able to do when they get to the Washington Monument?

   a. Take the elevator up to the top. b. Get to the observation level.

   c. Take pictures from high up. d. All of the above.

4. Which of the following can NOT be learnt from the recording?

   a. Madison Drive is a street.

   b. The tourists have just visited Capitol Hill.

   c. The Air and Space Museum and the National Gallery are not on the same side of the street.

   d. The Mall is a park.

5. What is the tour route?
   a. Capitol Hill — the Washington Monument — the White House.
   b. The Capitol Building — the National Gallery — the Washington Monument.
   c. The Washington Monument — the Mall — the Air & Space Museum.
   d. The Washington Monument — Capitol Hill — the White House.

### Exercise 2

**Listen again and complete the chart with information about the given places of interest.**

| Places of Interest in Washington D.C. | |
|---|---|
| the Capitol Building | opened in 1) *1800*; 2) *burned down* by the British during 3) *the War of 1812*; had to be completely 4) *rebuilt* |
| the National Gallery | has a collection of 5) *European and American art* from 6) *the 13th* to the 20th centuries |
| the Mall | 7) *park-like*; extends from 8) *the Capitol to the Washington Monument* |
| the Washington Monument | 9) *555* feet high; built in 10) *1884* |

## Part B Speaking Activities

### 1. Pair Work

*Listen to the recording again and pay attention to the language the tour guide used in introducing Washington, D.C. to the tourists. Answer the following questions orally. You may use the information you've got from what the tour guide says.*

1) What do you know about the Capitol Building and the Washington Monument?
2) Say something about the National Air and Space Museum.
3) What can you see on the way from the Capitol Building to the Washington Monument?

## 2. Communicative Function: Describing Places

Every one of us has been to places other than our home town. Every place that we have visited, whether it is a country, a city, a town, a neighborhood, a village, or even a building, has left certain impressions on our minds. We retain in our memory its unique characteristics that distinguish it from other places. In our daily conversation, we often find ourselves describing places to others. In doing so, we would initially focus on where the place is and what it is like. Then we would add other information about the place, such as its history, culture as well as things visitors can see and do in order to make our description more interesting and informative. How do you describe the location of a place? How do you describe the physical appearance of a place, say, the landscape of an area or the style of architecture of a building? How do you describe the historical, cultural, economic, scientific or other characteristics that contribute to the unique character and appeal of a place? In the box below, you'll find some sentences and structures that you may find useful when describing places.

### DESCRIBING PLACES

**Location**

The park is located / situated in the east of the island.

The temple is / lies in the south of the town.

The small town lies just north of the river.

The Botanic Garden is about three kilometers northeast of the town center.

The zoo is located to the north of the Botanic Garden.

The village is about fifty miles to the west of our university.

The museum is on Park Road, about ten minutes' walk from our college / within walking distance / just a short stroll from here.

The concert hall is situated next to a large shopping mall / at the foot of a hill / at the end of the road /opposite the Science Museum / at the corner of Main Street and River Road.

**Landscape and Architecture**

The city is surrounded by mountains on three sides and faces the sea to the east.

It's a coastal city with beautiful beaches and modern hotels / a historical town with narrow streets and ancient buildings / a typical water town surrounded

and crisscrossed by waterways / an area of countryside with rolling hills and quiet villages ...

There is a fountain in the middle of the square. On the east the square is dominated by a giant bronze statue and on the west by cafes and restaurants.

The pagoda has eight sides and stands about 60 meters high / at a height of about 60 meters.

The temple was built entirely of wood. It was so built that not a single nail was used in its construction.

The house is an example of typical Ming Dynasty architecture.

**Other Characteristics**

It's a lovely / quiet / peaceful little town with a laid-back atmosphere.

It's a very cosmopolitan / scenic / touristy city with plenty for tourists to see and do.

The city is famous for its ancient gardens / its waterways and bridges / its scenic beauty and pleasant weather / its long history and rich culture ...

The city boasts many historical sites/the best aquarium in the country / the oldest and largest museum in Asia / a thriving fashion industry ...

One of the attractions of the town is a Buddhist temple that was built during / that dates back to the Song Dynasty.

The museum houses / displays / features / contains a collection of ancient Chinese furniture.

## A Model

**Steve (an overseas student)** Hey, Beth. I'm going to Shanghai next week for a workshop there. I'm hoping to do some sightseeing as well. You're from the city. What places would you recommend that I visit?

**Beth** There are quite a few sights worth visiting in Shanghai. Let me first give you a brief sketch of its geography. The city is divided by the Huangpu River into two areas: Pudong and Puxi. Pudong, which means east of the Huangpu River, is the city's new financial district, and Puxi, which means west of the Huangpu River, is the older part of the city. Most of the tourist attractions are in Puxi, however.

**Steve** I hear the Bund is a must-see. Is it in Puxi?

**Beth** Yes. The Bund is actually a section of a road that runs along the west bank of the Huangpu River. It's famous for the old European-style buildings that line the west side of the road.

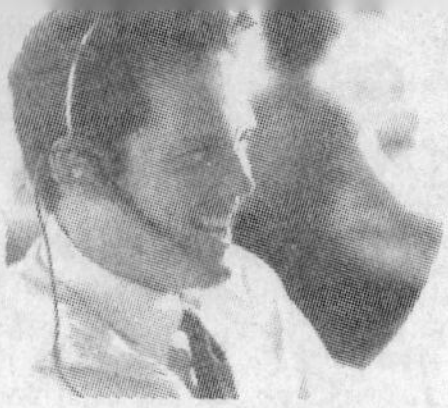



Most of these buildings were built in the 1920s and 1930s and represent a variety of architectural styles, giving the place the nickname "a museum of international architecture."

**Steve** Interesting.

**Beth** These buildings are a reminder of Shanghai's colonial past. They are a sharp contrast with the modern skyscrapers and high-rises that make up the skyline of Pudong just across the river. The Bund is the best place where you can have a good view of the Pudong skyline, which includes the Oriental Pearl TV Tower and the 88-story Jin Mao Tower.

**Steve** I've seen pictures of the Oriental Pearl Tower. I know it's the tallest TV tower in Asia.

**Beth** Right. The best time to see the Bund is at night when the lights on both sides of the river are on and the view is just fantastic.

**Steve** I bet it is.

**Beth** And if you want to take some souvenirs back from Shanghai, you can go to Nanjing Road, which is lined with shops on both sides. And it's only about a ten-minute's walk from the Bund.

**Steve** That's good. I would certainly like to take a walk along the road and do some shopping. By the way, Beth, are there other places in the vicinity of the Bund that are worth visiting?

**Beth** Sure, the Yuyuan Garden, which is just a few blocks south of the Bund. It's a beautiful traditional Chinese garden with a history of more than 400 years. This place is known as a shopping paradise to visitors. You can buy almost anything, from traditional Chinese arts and crafts, jewelry, to Chinese herbal medicines.

**Steve** That's great.

**Beth** A famous landmark in this area is a two-story teahouse located in the middle of a small lake.

**Steve** In the middle of a lake?

**Beth** Yes. It's called the Huxinting Teahouse and is reached via a bridge with nine turns. Even Queen Elizabeth II had tea there when she visited the Yuyuan Garden.

**Steve** Really! I've got to check this place out when I go there.

**Beth** You won't miss it. Just look for the zigzag bridge and the teahouse is right there in the middle of the lake.

**Steve** Great!

*Now make similar conversations of your own, using the given situations. Try to use in your conversations what you've learned in this lesson.*

**Situations:**

1) You are a tour guide, introducing Washington, D.C. to a group of tourists. Below is a map showing the places you would like to introduce to the tourists. You can start the tour from Capitol Hill.

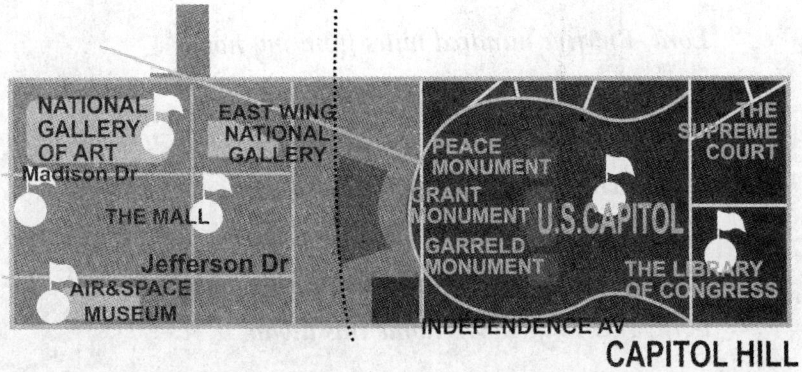


2) A foreign friend of yours plans to visit your hometown (or a place you're familiar with) for sightseeing. Describe to your friend the sights and attractions that you think are worth visiting in the place. Mention the location of every place of interest, what its main attractions are, and what your friend can do at the place.

# Part C Listen and Relax

## A Song

**Listen to the song *500 Miles* and sing along.**

### *500 Miles*

*If you miss the train I'm on,*
*You will know that I am gone.*
*You can hear the whistle blow a hundred miles,*
*A hundred miles, a hundred miles, a hundred miles, a hundred miles.*
*You can hear the whistle blow a hundred miles.*

*Lord, I'm one. Lord, I'm two. Lord, I'm three. Lord, I'm four.*
*Lord, I'm five hundred miles from my home.*
*Away from home, away from home, away from home, away from home,*

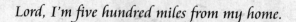

*Lord, I'm five hundred miles from my home.*

*Not a shirt on my back,*
*Not a penny to my name.*
*Lord, I can't go down home this away,*
*This away, this away, this away, this away.*
*Lord, I can't go down home this away.*

# Part D Further Listening

## Passage 1

### The Library of Congress

**Exercise**

**You are going to hear a passage. Listen carefully and choose the right answer to each question you hear.**

The Library of Congress is the national library of the United States. It was founded in 1800 to serve the needs of the congressmen. Today, the Library of Congress contains books, articles and documents on every subject imaginable, in addition to congressional records. Besides senators, congressmen and other government officials, it serves libraries, researchers, artists and scientists throughout the country and the world.

The Library of Congress is one of the largest libraries in the world. It has a collection of 74 million items which are housed in three buildings. The Library is open to the public, but not everyone has borrowing privileges. Magazines, manuscripts, maps, music, newspapers and photographs fill the stacks. The bookshelves stretch for 350 miles. Of the 18 million books, more than half are in languages other than English.

The main reading room is a great hall with marble pillars. It is the center of activity in the library. There is a computer catalog center with six terminals for quick access to information. For greater speed and efficiency, the library has installed an electric book-carrying system that carries books from one building to another in only a few seconds.

The Library of Congress also offers a wide variety of cultural programs. For example, it sponsors chamber music concerts, poetry festivals, lectures and readings. The Library of Congress is always expanding to meet the needs of the modern world.

1. What was the original purpose of building the Library of Congress?
   a. To serve researchers' needs.
   b. To serve scientists' needs.
   c. To serve congressmen's needs.
   d. All of the above.

2. How many books does the speaker say the library has?
   a. 74 million.
   b. 70 million.
   c. 350 million.
   d. 18 million.

3. Which of the following is NOT mentioned about the main reading room?
   a. It is located in the center of the library.
   b. It has a computer center.
   c. It has marble pillars.
   d. It is a large hall.

4. Which group of cultural programs does the library offer according to the passage?
   a. Concerts and film festivals.
   b. Lectures and art shows.
   c. Lectures and readings.
   d. Concerts and play readings.

5. What can we learn about the Library of Congress?
   a. It has a history of over 200 years.
   b. It is the largest library in the world.
   c. Every citizen can borrow books from the library.
   d. It has connections with various libraries in the world.

## Passage 2

# The Statue of Liberty

### Exercise

**Listen to the passage carefully and choose the right answer to each question you hear.**

The Statue of Liberty is located on Ellis Island in New York Harbor. It was designed by a French sculptor named Bartholdi and was given to the U.S. by France in 1886 to celebrate the 100th anniversary of U.S. Independence.

After years and years of acid rain, the Statue had spots on her copper skin. Her iron neck and shoulders were weakening. Her torch leaked. Her gown was rusted. And hundreds of iron bars that held the skin to her skeleton were eroding. American school children were asked to collect money to help fix up the Statue.

The most important repair was the replacement of more than 2,000 two-inch-wide iron bars holding the outer sheets of copper to her skeleton. They were replaced with metal bars that wouldn't cause electrolysis with copper. The most dramatic change was the work done on the torch. Workers took the torch off and completely reconstructed it. The old torch was put in a museum in the basement of the Statue. So with a lot of hard work and millions of dollars from people all across the U.S., Miss Liberty is now once again lifting high her torch of freedom and standing proudly on Ellis Island.

1. What is the passage mainly about?
   a. The history of the Statue of Liberty.
   b. The reconstruction of the Statue of Liberty.
   c. The repair of the Statue of Liberty.
   d. The reconstruction of the torch of the Statue of Liberty.

2. What metal forms the skin of the Statue of Liberty?
   a. Iron.
   b. Copper.
   c. Steel.
   d. Zinc.

3. What was the most important work done on the Statue?
   a. Taking off the torch.
   b. Reconstructing the torch.

c. Replacing the neck, shoulders and iron bars of the Statue.

d. Replacing the iron bars.

4. What did the Americans do to the old torch?

a. They had it repainted.

b. They had it repaired.

c. They put it in the basement of a museum.

d. They put it in a museum on Ellis Island.

5. Which of the following statements can NOT be inferred from the passage?

a. The Statue was showing her age.

b. The torch was the most seriously damaged part of the Statue.

c. American school children contributed a lot to the repair of the Statue.

d. Acid rain does great damage to metal.

# Part E Home Listening

## Passage 1

## Midnight Ride

### Exercise

**Listen to the passage and fill in the following chart with the information you get from the recording.**

Professor Ken Guest is a cultural anthropologist. He leads the all-night bike tour through Manhattan each spring as part of his college course "The People of New York". This year's tour, held on May 4 and 5, was his fourth one.

The tour offers vivid illustration of in-class work, which explores the role immigration and migration have played and continue to play in shaping the city's identity. Topics include why people

have been drawn to New York; the different ways that religion, culture, gender, race, and ethnicity have shaped the city's population; and the impact of newcomers on urban culture, politics, and the economy.

This year's tour began at Columbia University and went on at a leisurely pace south through Manhattan, with stops in various neighborhoods. The group of 14 cyclists stopped among other places at Manhattan Valley, Central Park, Rockefeller Center, Times Square, City Hall, the World Trade Center Site, Wall Street, Little Italy, Chinatown, where the group dined at Chinatown's famous restaurant Wo Hop's. A happy and bleary-eyed group witnessed the sunrise from the Brooklyn Bridge — exactly on schedule — at 5:51 a.m.

The idea of the tour was inspired by a similar tour Professor Guest took as an undergraduate. He said, "When I was an undergraduate at Columbia, my teacher Professor Kenneth Jackson led an all-night bike tour of New York. It was so memorable and so much fun." Professor Guest's students are equally charmed by this tour. He said, "The kids' reactions have been fantastic. It's a big hit. It's a thrilling experience to see New York City at night. You get a vastly different sense of the city and its life during these hours. The city is surprisingly empty between midnight and 6; it's a beautiful time. And what a perfect activity for getting students out of the classroom and into the city."

| This Year's All-Night Bike Tour | |
|---|---|
| Leader | Professor Ken Guest |
| Date | 1) *May 4 and 5* |
| Route | Began at 2) *Columbia University* and went 3) *south* through 4) *Manhattan* |
| Participants | 5) *14* students on their bikes |
| Stops | 6) *Manhattan Valley*, 7) *Central Park*, Rockefeller Center, 8) *Times Square*, City Hall, the World Trade Center Cite, Wall Street, Little Italy, 9) *Chinatown* |
| Place to see the sunrise | The Brooklyn Bridge |
| Time to see the sunrise | 10) *5:51 a.m.* |
| Students' reactions | It's a 11) *big hit*. It's a thrilling experience to 12) *see New York City at night*. |
| Professor Guest's remarks | It is a perfect activity for 13) *getting students out of the classroom* and 14) *into the city*. |

## Passage 2

# Moscow — the Most Expensive City in the World

### Exercise

**Listen to the passage and write down your answers to the following questions.**

The 2007 Cost of Living Survey by Mercer was released last Monday. The survey ranked 143 cities around the world. It compared those cities by a cost of living index for 200 items, such as housing, transportation and food costs. The findings are designed to help multinational employers determine compensation for the workers they have sent abroad.

According to the survey, Moscow is the world's most expensive city for the second year in a row, thanks to a rising ruble and high housing costs. The index for Moscow rose from 123.9 in 2006 to 134.4 this year, against 100 for New York. The cost of living for foreigners in the Russian capital is nearly 35 percent higher than in New York, which served as the base city for the survey released Monday. In Moscow, a luxury two-bedroom apartment will cost a foreigner $4,000 a month; a CD rings up at $24.83; one copy of an international daily newspaper is $6.30; and a fast-food hamburger meal totals $4.80.

London came second at 126.3, up from fifth last year. The rising pound and the euro against the U.S. dollar on the foreign exchange market helped 30 European cities to top spots on the 2007 list. Copenhagen, Geneva, Zurich and Oslo, respectively, were placed among the top 10.

South Korea's Seoul fell from second to third place with an index reading of 122.4, replacing Tokyo, which slid to fourth place at 122.1, followed by Hong Kong.

Osaka, Japan's second-biggest city, ranked eighth, down from sixth last year.

The rankings of Chinese cities, which showed rapid advances in last year's survey, dropped. Beijing and Shanghai took the 20th and 26th places respectively, due mainly to stabilized housing costs.

New York and Los Angeles were the only two North American cities to rank among the highest 50, though both fell in the rankings. The Big Apple dropped five places to No. 15, while Los Angeles fell to No. 42 from No. 29 in 2006.

Ranking as the least expensive city for the fifth year in a row was Paraguay's capital of Asuncion, where the cost of living is half that of New York.

1. Why is Moscow ranked as the world's most expensive city?
   Give at least three examples.
   1) <u>*The cost of living for foreigners is nearly 35% higher than in New York*</u>.
   2) <u>*A luxury two-bedroom apartment costs $4,000 a month*</u>.
   3) <u>*A CD costs $24.83*</u>.
2. What cities are placed among the top 10 besides Moscow? Name at least 5 cities.
   <u>*London, Seoul, Hong Kong, Geneva, Osaka ...*</u>
3. What places do Beijing and Shanghai take?
   <u>*Beijing took the 20th place; Shanghai the 26th place*</u>.
4. What is the cost of living in Paraguay's capital of Asuncion — the least expensive city in the world? The cost of living there is <u>*half that of New York*</u>.

# Unit 3

## An Inquiry

## Part A Listening Activities

### A Conversation

## Job Application

**W** Good morning.

**M** Er, good morning, yes, er ...

**W** I'm phoning about the job that was in the paper last night.

**M** Oh yes, yes, erm, well, could you tell me your name, please?

**W** Oh, Candida Fawcett.

**M** Oh, yes. Erm, well, what exactly, er, is it that interests you about the, about the job?

**W** Well, I just thought that it was right up my street, you know.

**M** Really, hmm. Erm, well, could you perhaps tell me a little about yourself?

**W** Yes, erm, I'm 23. I've been working abroad. I um ...

**M** Where exactly have you been working, please?

**W** Oh, in Geneva.

**M** Oh, really?

**W** Yes.

**M** And, what were you doing there?

**W** Oh, secretarial work.

**M** I see.

**W** And erm, previous to that, I was at a university.

**M** Hmmm ... hm.

**W** And erm ...

**M** Which university was that?

**W** Oh, the University of Manchester. I've got a degree in English.

**M** Hmm, hmm. And er, you're interested in the job?

**W** Oh, yes sir, really, I am. Erm, can you tell me what it's paying?

**M** Er, well, I think that would be negotiable, erm, if we decide to invite you for interview then I should, er, I should er, er talk to you about that, but perhaps you could give me an idea of what sort of er ...

**W** Oh, I'm ...

**M** What sort of er range you're interested in?

**W** I'm not really too worried about getting a ... er ... large salary to start with.

**M** Really?

**W** It's just that I should be, you know, very happy, to be able to have a job, to come back to England and work and er ...

**M** Do you have any special reasons for wanting to come back?

**W** Well, it's just that with being, working in Geneva for a year and I sort of thought it would be nice to be nearer to the family, you know.

**M** I see. Yes. And, er, how do you see this job developing?

**W** Well, I am ambitious. I, I, you know, I do hope that my career as a secretary will lead me eventually into management or, or ...

**M** I see. You, you have, you have foreign languages, I take it.

**W** Oh yes, sir, yes sir, French and Italian.

**M** Oh yes, hmmmm. Well, look, I think the best thing for you to do is to, is to reply in writing to the advertisement and er ...

**W** Oh, can't I arrange for an interview now?

**M** Well, I'm afraid, we must wait until all the, all the applications are in, in writing and er, er we'll then decide er on a short list and er, if you're on the short list, of course we shall see

you.

**W** Oh, I see.

**M** Yes, so, I'll look forward to receiving your er, your application in writing in the next day or two.

**W** Oh, yes, yes, certainly.

**M** Yes, thank you very much, goodbye.

**W** Thank you. Goodbye.

## New Words and Expressions

| | | | |
|---|---|---|---|
| secretarial | /ˌsekrəˈteərɪəl/ | *adj.* | 秘书的 (of or relating to) a secretary or a secretary's work |
| negotiable | /nɪˈgəʊʃɪəbl/ | *adj.* | 可磋商的 can be negotiated |
| range | /reɪndʒ/ | *n.* | （有效）范围，幅度 the extent to which variation is possible |
| eventually | /ɪˈventjʊəlɪ/ | *adv.* | 最终 finally |
| be right up one's street | | | 正中某人意的 (*BrE, informal*) to be in keeping with or satisfying one's abilities, interests, or tastes |
| to start with | | | 一开始 at the beginning |
| I take it … | | | 我认为…… I think |
| on the short list | | | 供最后挑选用的候选人名单 on the list of those people preferred or most likely to be chosen |
| Candida Fawcett | /ˈkændɪdə ˈfɔːset/ | | （女子名） a woman's full name |

## Language and Culture Notes

1. ***Background Information***

Various kinds of advertisements can be found in newspapers every day. Many of these ads deal with employment. Each job advertisement may contain a brief description of the job; requirements of the applicants (sex, age, qualifications, working experience, health condition,

etc.) and advantages of the job (pay, holiday, etc.). To apply for a job, one has to send in a formal letter of application which must contain a statement of one's qualifications and working experience, reasons for wanting the job and reasons why one is most suitable for the job, letters of recommendation and availability for interview. Some people may also make inquiries about a job by telephone but an informal phone call cannot replace a written statement of application. If a person's application is approved, he will receive a notice for an interview during which the applicant will be asked questions in relation to his qualifications for the job he wishes to take. At the end of the interview he may be informed whether his application is accepted or not.

2. ***be up one's street*** (*colloq.*) to be within one's area of knowledge, interest, etc.

## Exercise 1

**Listen to the conversation and choose the right answer to each question you hear.**

1. What are the two speakers doing?
   a. Arranging an interview.
   b. Having an interview.
   c. Meeting in the street and talking about job application.
   d. Talking on the phone about a job advertised in the paper.

2. Why is the woman applying for this job?
   a. Because it is interesting.
   b. Because the pay is negotiable.
   c. Because she wants to get back to England.
   d. Because she needs money, and the pay for the job is handsome.

3. Why did the woman want to come back from abroad?
   a. She wanted to be nearer to her family.
   b. She thought her ambition would be easier to achieve at home.
   c. She got bored living and working abroad.
   d. She thought she would be able to find a better job at home.

4. What would the woman probably do in the next few days?
   a. Wait for the man to call her back.
   b. Write a written application for the job.
   c. Write a short list of interviews to be held.

d. Call the manager for confirmation of the job.

5. What conclusion can you draw from the conversation?
   a. The man is satisfied with the woman's qualifications.
   b. The man is not satisfied with the woman's qualifications.
   c. People can find better jobs at home than abroad.
   d. The woman is homesick.

### Exercise 2

**Listen to the conversation again and write down your answers to the following questions.**

1. What advantages does the woman have in applying for the job?
   a. *Experience of working abroad for a year.*
   b. *Experience of working as a secretary abroad.*
   c. *A university degree in English.*
   d. *Foreign languages (French and Italian).*
2. What is the woman's ambition?
   *To get into management work.*

## Part B Speaking Activities

**Pair Work**

### Exercise 1

**Work in pairs. Make a dialogue on the topic "A Job after Graduation". The following questions may be helpful to you.**

1. What kind of job would you like to have after graduation?

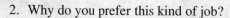

2. Why do you prefer this kind of job?
3. What advantages do you think you have in applying for the job?
4. What is your ambition in work?
5. What would you do if you fail to get the job you want?

### Exercise 2

**Suppose you are about to graduate and are looking for a job. You have sent your applications to a company and have landed an interview. Preparation is key to a successful job interview. Read the following interview questions and think about how you would answer them.**

1. Tell me about yourself.
2. How would your friends describe you?
3. Why do you want to work here?
4. What do you think makes you qualified for this position?
5. What courses did you study at college? In what ways have your college experiences prepared you for this position?
6. What can you bring to the company if you become one of its members?
7. What are your strengths and weaknesses?
8. How would you deal with a difficult situation?
9. What are your goals for the next five years?

*Now work in pairs and role-play the interview. Take turns to play the part of the interviewer and that of the interviewee.*

## Part C Listen and Relax

### Jokes

**Here are some jokes about jobs. Listen and enjoy.**

1. My wife has a very responsible job. If anything goes wrong, she's responsible.

2. The best job for people who think they are paranoid(多疑的) is drive a taxi — then they really will always have people talking behind their backs.
3. A young student was desperate for money and so in his vacation he decided to take a job in a local factory as it paid good wages.

   "Now," said the supervisor, "your first job is to sweep the floor."

   "But I've got a BA degree," said the student, "and I'm currently studying for a master's in business administration."

   "Oh!" said the supervisor. "In that case I'd better show you how to hold the broom."
4. When I left university I went for several job interviews. At the first interview I was turned down because I wasn't married. The personnel officer said that married men had much more experience of knowing how to cope if a boss shouted at them.

# Part D Further Listening

## A Passage

### A Career Counseling Office

#### Exercise

**Listen to the passage carefully and choose the right answer to each question you hear.**

When American students graduate from college, they must find jobs for themselves. But often they get help from their college and university. Every college has a career counseling office. The people who work there help students learn about different kinds of jobs and the chances for employment. Students can discuss these with a counselor during their first year of college. Some use the information a counselor gives them when deciding what subjects to study.

For example, a girl student wants to be an engineer, but she does not know what kind. The counselor can tell the girl that, when she graduates in four years, there will be more jobs for structural engineers than for chemical engineers. Therefore, the student may decide to study structural engineering. The career counseling office also communicates with local and national companies.

Company officials sometimes visit the university to talk to students who want to work for them. The career counseling offices arrange these meetings for the company and the students. They also have classes for students. They teach the students how to find a job, such as what to say to company officials and how to write letters telling about themselves.

Experts say that American students who are employed when they finish college usually find jobs in their own field of study. Those who must search for months after graduation usually take lower paid jobs, and their jobs are not connected to what they studied in college. The experts foretell that in the coming years there will be more jobs for health workers, financial experts, teachers and computer scientists.

1. How do American students find jobs when they graduate from college?
   a. By themselves.
   b. With the help of career counseling agencies.
   c. With the help of local companies.
   d. With the help of their parents.

2. What information can students get from the career counselor?
   a. The job situation of the year.
   b. A description of different kinds of jobs and chances for employment.
   c. Comparison of the advantages of different jobs.
   d. A description of the jobs available.

3. What else does the career counseling office do to help students?
   a. It arranges visits to local and national companies.
   b. It helps most students choose what subjects to study.
   c. It arranges meetings for the companies and the students who want to work for them.
   d. It writes letters of recommendation to the companies for the students.

4. What jobs are usually taken by American students who are employed immediately after leaving college?
   a. Jobs in health work, finance, teaching and computer science.
   b. Jobs having little connection with the subjects they've studied.
   c. Jobs in research work.
   d. Jobs in their own field of study.

5. What can you conclude from the passage?
   a. American students prefer jobs with higher pay.
   b. Lower paid jobs actually take longer to find.

c. The career counseling offices do a good job.

d. Most students can find jobs as soon as they leave college.

## A Conversation

### I Sure Hope That I Can Work Here

**Exercise**

**Listen to the conversation carefully. Then supply the missing information in the chart.**

**W** Please sit down. Let's see, you're Mr Stone, is that right?

**M** Yes. I'm Bob Stone.

**W** And you're looking for a job, aren't you?

**M** Yes, I am. I'll graduate from college in June. I'm majoring in architecture.

**W** I see. Have you ever done any work in this field?

**M** No, nothing. We did some practice work in class, though.

**W** Do you have copies of your letters of recommendation with you?

**M** Yes. One's from Dr Hilton and one's from Mr Phelps.

**W** Good. Now what kind of salary are you hoping to get?

**M** From what I've read it seems that a starting salary would be around $20,000 a year.

**W** Here you would start at $15,000 for the first year — a kind of training period. Then you would go to $18,000. After that your raises would depend on how well you worked.

**M** That sounds fair enough. What about other benefits, things like vacation?

**W** Those are all explained in this pamphlet. You can take it along and look at it at home.

**M** Is it all right if I send in the rest of the things for my application?

**W** That would be fine. After Mr Johnson looks all the applications over he'll make the final decision.

**M** What do you think the chances are I'll get a job?

**W** Well, I'm talking to three people today and four tomorrow. We'll be hiring two people.

**M** I sure hope that I can work here. But I guess I'll just have to go home and wait.

**W** You'll hear sometime next month. Good luck and thanks for coming in today.

| Information of the Applicant | |
|---|---|
| **Name** | *Bob Stone* |
| **Major** | *Architecture* |
| **Work Experience** | *None except some practice work in class* |
| **Letters of Recommendation** | *Two*, one from Dr Hilton and the other from Mr Phelps |
| **Qualifications** | College graduate |
| **Expectations** | *Starting salary* — around *$20,000* a year; benefits — like *vacation* |

# Part E Home Listening

## Conversation 1

### A Job Interview

#### Exercise

**Listen to the job interview and choose the right answer to each question you hear.**

**M** Hi, I'm Tim Li. Welcome.

**W** Hi, I'm Tina Green.

**M** Miss or Mrs?

**W** Miss.

**M** Please have a seat, Miss Green. Thanks for coming in. Did you bring your resume?

**W** Yes. Here you are.

**M** Great. First of all, let me tell you a little bit about the job. We're looking for someone to sell our new software product internationally. The job requires flexibility, independence and most importantly, a pleasant manner with customers.

**W** I know … that's really important. You know I've worked in sales for years and have always tried to really listen to my customers to find out what they need. I think I'm really good at that.

**M** That's great. So could you tell me a little bit about your experience with software programs?

**W** Sure. Well, I've trained people how to use a similar software product for the past two years at my current job, so I really feel I know the product and customer needs.

**M** Hmm… very interesting, and what about your sales experience?

**W** I've been with my present company for about three years and in my present position since last year. During the past three years I've been named salesperson of the month three times, and have taken top sales awards several times as well.

**M** Very impressive, Miss Green.

**W** I'm also taking graduate courses right now in marketing. I feel it really helps me understand the market better, especially the competition.

**M** You've been very busy, Miss Green. Well, thanks very much for coming in. We'll be in touch then.

1. What kind of job is Miss Green applying for?
   a. In sales.
   b. In management.
   c. In marketing.
   d. In software product engineering.

2. What has Miss Green been doing at her present job?
   a. Dealing with complaints from customers.
   b. Designing software products.
   c. Training people how to use a software product.
   d. Selling software products internationally.

3. What is the most important quality that an applicant for the job needs according to the man?
   a. Flexibility.
   b. Independence.
   c. A lot of experience in sales.
   d. A pleasant manner with customers.

4. What can you learn about Miss Green from the conversation?
   a. She's really good at listening to customers.
   b. She has a lot of experience in training sales personnel.
   c. She's the best salesperson in her present company.
   d. She's left her job to study graduate courses in marketing at college.

5. What can you infer from the conversation?
   a. Miss Green will be able to do the job after a period of training.

b. Miss Green seems the right person for the job.

c. The man is hesitating whether to accept Miss Green or not.

d. The man does not think Miss Green is qualified.

## Conversation 2

# A Survey

### Exercise

**Listen to the conversation and write down your answers to the following questions.**

**M** Excuse me, madam. I'm a reporter for Channel 9 and we're doing a survey on the choices people make. Would you mind if I asked you a couple of questions?

**W** Uh huh, but what do you mean by choices?

**M** Well, let's take something simple like a choice you've made in your life that you're particularly glad about.

**W** OK. Um … yes. There is. Oh, I'm glad that I married my husband. That was definitely a good choice.

**M** Well, that's nice to hear, especially these days. OK, let's look at it the other way. Is there anything you've done that you wish you hadn't done?

**W** Oh, goodness me yes! Right now I really wish I hadn't given my son an electric guitar for his birthday.

**M** Noisy, huh?

**W** You can say that again. I guess if I hadn't given it to him I would still be able to get some sleep. Sometimes he plays all night long.

**M** Yeah, kids. What can you do? So, anything else? How about something you didn't do that you wish you had done?

**W** Let me see. Yeah. I was offered a job once in Paris. I kind of wish I had taken it, but I didn't. I was just out of college and my parents didn't want me to move overseas. If I had gone I would have been able to travel in Europe and I would have learned French. But I did meet my future husband instead, so it wasn't all bad.

**M** No, I guess not. Well, thanks a lot for your time.

**W** Not at all.

1. What is the woman glad about?
   *She's glad that she married her husband, which is definitely a good choice.*
2. What is the thing that the woman has done but wishes she hadn't done?
   *The woman wishes that she hadn't bought her son an electric guitar for his birthday.*
3. Is there something that the woman didn't do but wished she had done?
   *Yes. She regrets a little that she didn't accept a job offer in Paris.*
4. How does she feel now about her decision not to take the job?
   *She thinks it wasn't all bad because if she had taken the job in Paris, she wouldn't have met her future husband.*

# Unit 4

# Health

## Part A Listening Activities

### A Forum

### Mercy Killing

Mr David Thomson is dying of cancer. He has been in a coma for more than five months and is being kept alive by a machine which supplies him with oxygen. His doctor John Williams says he has no chance of recovery. His wife has applied to a court for permission to have the machine switched off.

**Mrs Thomson** My husband has been reduced to the condition of a vegetable. Keeping him alive is meaningless now. I'm sure that if he could speak, he would beg us to switch off that machine. Why can't he die with dignity? Seeing him in this condition is causing us all great suffering.

**Dr Williams** Mr Thomson is clinically alive, but he has absolutely no chance of recovery.

His brain had been irreparably damaged by the coma. He could remain in this condition for years. Frankly speaking, that would benefit nobody. Hospital beds are scarce and medical staff are very busy. Hundreds of patients are waiting to be treated. It would be wrong to keep Mr Thomson here and to refuse other patients who do have a chance of recovery. If his relatives request us to do so, and if the court gives us permission, we will terminate the treatment and allow him to die a natural death.

**Dr Nelson** I'm very surprised that Dr Williams approves of Mrs Thomson's court application. A doctor's duty is to preserve life in whatever way he can. Not to do so is a betrayal of his patient's trust and may amount to professional negligence. A doctor can never state categorically that his patient has no chance of recovery, however bad the situation may seem. I've seen comatose patients suddenly regain consciousness after several months and become relatively healthy again. Human life is far too precious to terminate for the convenience of others.

**Robert Harriman, M.P.** Right now, there are thousands of incurable patients lying helplessly in bed, suffering pain and misery and wishing they could be allowed to die. But the doctors are afraid to facilitate their deaths for fear of legal or professional repercussions. I propose that doctors be allowed to discontinue treatment or administer lethal doses of painkillers if requested to do so by patients suffering from incurable diseases, or, in the case of comatose patients, by their relatives. It's time the law recognized the fact that people not only have a right to live, they also have a right to die.

**Richard Brake, Lawyer** Any doctor who, with the intention of terminating the life of a patient, performs acts which lead to the death of the patient, may be convicted of murder, under the present law. No court is empowered to authorize such acts and therefore Mrs Thomson's application is to be rejected.

## New Words and Expressions

| | | | |
|---|---|---|---|
| coma | /ˈkəʊmə/ | *n.* | 昏迷 a state of being unconscious |
| oxygen | /ˈɒksɪdʒən/ | *n.* | 氧 a chemical element that forms a large part of the air on earth |
| vegetable | /ˈvedʒɪtəbl/ | *n.* | 植物人 a person who is completely |

| | | | |
|---|---|---|---|
| | | | unable to move and to react, usually because of brain damage |
| dignity | /ˈdɪgnətɪ/ | *n.* | 尊严 the quality or state of being worthy of respect |
| clinically | /ˈklɪnɪkəlɪ/ | *adv.* | 临床 in a clinical manner |
| irreparably | /ɪˈrepərəblɪ/ | *adv.* | 无可挽救地 in the manner of being impossible to repair or mend |
| terminate | /ˈtɜːmɪneɪt/ | *v.* | 终止 to put an end to |
| betrayal | /bɪˈtreɪəl/ | *n.* | 辜负，失信于 disloyalty, departure from the hopes or expectations of others |
| comatose | /ˈkəʊmətəʊs/ | *adj.* | 昏迷的 in a state of coma |
| categorically | /ˌkætɪˈgɒrɪkəlɪ/ | *adv.* | 绝对地 absolutely |
| facilitate | /fəˈsɪlɪteɪt/ | *v.* | 使容易 to make easier or less difficult |
| repercussion | /ˌriːpəˈkʌʃən/ | *n.* | 反响 an effect or result, often indirect or remote, of some event or action |
| administer | /ədˈmɪnɪstə(r)/ | *v.* | 给(病人服药) to give (medicine to a patient) |
| lethal | /ˈliːθəl/ | *adj.* | 致命的 fatal |
| painkiller | /ˈpeɪnˌkɪlə(r)/ | *n.* | 止痛药 a drug that relieves pain |
| empower | /ɪmˈpaʊə(r)/ | *v.* | 授权，准许 to give power to, or to authorize by legal or official means |
| authorize | /ˈɔːθəraɪz/ | *v.* | 批准，认可 to give official power to |

---

| | | |
|---|---|---|
| mercy killing | /ˈmɜːsɪ/ | 安乐死 the act of killing someone painlessly |
| approve of | | 赞同 to consent or agree to |
| amount to | | (在效果方面)等同 to be equal to |
| professional negligence | /ˈneglɪdʒəns/ | 失职 failing to give enough attention to one's responsibilities as a doctor, lawyer, etc. |
| be convicted of | /kənˈvɪktɪd/ | 被证明有……罪 to prove or declare guilty of an offense, esp. after a legal trial |

## Language and Culture Notes

***Background Information*** Mercy killing means to give a human being easy and painless death for the sake of mercy. Some people hold that for patients with painful and terminal diseases mercy killing is a solution, for it will allow them to die a peaceful death and it seems to benefit everybody: the patients themselves, their relatives, the medical staff, and other patients who are waiting for hospital beds. But mercy killing is still a controversial issue. Those who are strongly against it hold that the possibility of abuse will expose sick people to all kinds of danger once it is legalized. At present, many societies and organizations have been formed in the world to promote mercy killing but only in Netherlands and Belgium has it been legalized. However, in the Netherlands the society and the courts tend to tolerate doctor-assisted suicide if strict criteria are met. (These are if the patient is competent, if he or she has repeatedly requested mercy killing, and is experiencing unbearable suffering.) In 1995 about 2.3% of all Dutch deaths, or 3,118 cases, were attributed to mercy killing by government studies. A few cases of mercy killing are also reported in the U.S. although the majority of the public are against it.

### Exercise 1

**Listen to the panel discussion and choose the right answer to each question you hear.**

1. What is Mrs Thomson's problem?
   a. She's suffering from some incurable illness.
   b. She can do nothing to help her husband.
   c. Her husband is in the condition of a vegetable.
   d. Her application to the court has been rejected.

2. How would Mrs Thomson like to have the problem resolved?
   a. To take her husband home.
   b. To terminate the meaningless treatment at once.
   c. To continue the treatment.
   d. To get the court's permission to terminate the treatment.

3. What was one of the reasons why Dr Williams said that keeping Mr Thomson in that condition would benefit nobody?
   a. Hospital beds should be provided only to patients whose diseases are curable.
   b. Mr Thomson had already suffered too much.

c. It is meaningless to prolong life when there is no chance of recovery.
d. It is a great waste of energy and money trying to prolong the life of patients in coma.

4. Which of the following is NOT mentioned as a kind of mercy killing?
   a. To administer an overdose of sleeping pills.
   b. To terminate treatment.
   c. To administer a lethal dose of painkillers.
   d. To switch off the machine that supplies oxygen.

5. What can be concluded from the discussion?
   a. Mercy killing is humane but should not be encouraged.
   b. To save more lives, it is important to develop new drugs rather than practice mercy killing.
   c. Mercy killing is not different from murder.
   d. It may take a long time before people can agree on mercy killing.

## Exercise 2

**Listen to the discussion again and write down in the table the different points of views of the participants.**

| Name of Participant | Does he or she approve of mercy killing? | His or her major arguments |
|---|---|---|
| Mrs Thomson | 1) Yes | 2) Keeping a comatose patient alive is *meaningless*. Seeing patients in this condition causes relatives *great suffering*. |
| Dr Williams | 3) Yes | 4) *To continue treatment to patients who have no chance of recovery* will benefit nobody. |
| Dr Nelson | 5) No | 6) A doctor's duty is *to preserve life in whatever way he can*, and not to do so is *a betrayal of his patients' trust* and may amount to *professional negligence*. |

| | | |
|---|---|---|
| **Robert Harriman, M.P.** | 7) Yes | 8) Doctors should be allowed to *discontinue treatment to those patients who are suffering from incurable diseases*. People not only have *a right to live*, but also *a right to die*. |
| **Richard Brake, Lawyer** | 9) No | 10) Under the present law, any doctor who performs *mercy killing may be convicted of murder*. |

# Part B Speaking Activities

## 1. Pair Work

*Answer the following questions. Base your answer on the information you've got from the listening material and on your own judgment.*

1) What is mercy killing?
   (On whom may it be performed?
   — patients with terminal diseases
   — patients in a long coma
   What could be done to perform mercy killing?
   — discontinue treatment
   — administer lethal doses of painkillers)
2) Do you approve of mercy killing? Why or why not?

## 2. Communicative Function: Talking About Health and Health-related Issues

Health is one of the most important aspects of our lives. It is the foundation of a happy and productive life. We all have the experience of how even a minor illness such as a cold or headache can be debilitating and make us feel weak and wretched. Health, of course, is more than just the absence of disease. Good health means a state of physical, mental and emotional well-being that enables us to function efficiently in the different roles that we play in life. Health is a topic that interests us all. But how do you express yourselves in talking about health and its related issues in English? How do you describe a person as healthy or unhealthy? What do you think contributes to good health? What changes in lifestyle can make people healthier? In the box below, you'll find some sentences and structures that you may find useful when talking about health and heath-related issues such as diet and exercise.

## TALKING ABOUT HEALTH AND HEALTH-RELATED ISSUES

A healthy diet and regular exercise are the building blocks of / are the key to good health.

Fast foods are typically high in / are full of / are loaded with fat, calories, sugar and salt.

Processed snacks tend to be low in fiber and nutrients, but high in salt and sugar / contain food additives (食品添加剂) that are harmful to our health.

Meat, dairy products and eggs contain saturated fats (饱和脂肪) that can increase the level of cholesterol (胆固醇) in our blood.

Plant products like vegetable oils, nuts and seeds contain unsaturated fats (不饱和脂肪) that can actually reduce the level of cholesterol in our blood.

Too much fat can raise your blood cholesterol levels and put you at a higher risk / increase your risk for heart disease, stroke, diabetes (糖尿病) and some types of cancer.

Poor / Unhealthy eating habits and too little exercise can lead to overweight and obesity (肥胖).

Many people tend to eat more when they are feeling bored / sad / angry / stressed.

You gain weight when the number of calories you eat is more than the number of calories your body uses.

If you skip meals during the day, you will be more likely to make up for those missing calories by snacking or eating more at the next meal.

The secret to weight loss is to choose healthy foods and take in fewer calories

than you burn.

A healthier way to lose weight is to eat many small meals throughout the day that include a variety of nutritious, low-fat, and low-calorie foods.

Try to eat a wide variety of food. No one food can provide us with all we need to keep our bodies healthy.

You can eat whatever you want as long as it's in moderation / as long as you take enough exercise.

A healthy and well-balanced diet can improve not only your energy level but also your appearance.

Exercise helps reduce stress, depression, and more importantly, the amount of fat stored in your body.

Regular exercise combined with a balanced diet is the best way to maintain a healthy body weight.

Sleep is just as important for overall health as diet and exercise.

Most adults need seven to eight hours of sleep each night to feel refreshed and function optimally during the day.

Sleep loss can have a negative effect on your physical and emotional health.

Studies show that there is a link between lack of sleep and weight gain / that people who get less sleep are at greater risk for heart disease and heart attacks.

A good night's sleep is often the best way to help you cope with stress, solve problems, or recover from illness.

Make sure you eat a wide variety of food, especially fruits and vegetables / you get enough sleep / you eat healthily and take regular exercise.

## A Model

**Pam** Carol, want some potato chips?

**Carol** Well … No, thank you.

**Pam** But aren't potato chips your favorite snack? Try some. They are very tasty.

**Carol** I know they are tasty, but they are also very unhealthy. You know they contain a lot of fat and salt and are high in calories.

**Pam** Come on, Carol. Since when have you become so health conscious?

**Carol** I watched a movie recently called *Super Size Me*. It is about a man who ate nothing but

McDonald's for a month, you know, three times a day, every day. And by the end of the month he gained more than 10 kilos and his health also deteriorated.

**Pam** Really? But wasn't he crazy? Who would eat at McDonald's three times a day and every day?

**Carol** It's a documentary film. The man simply used himself as a guinea pig to test the effects of fast food on the human body. And the point of the movie is very clear: Fast foods are bad, even in moderation.

**Pam** I know, but they are delicious. I love McDonald's, especially their French fries. Don't you think it's unfair that something so tasty can be so bad to you?

**Carol** I think it's OK if you eat at McDonald's once in a while. You don't have to avoid eating there completely. Just don't eat French fries too often. After watching the movie, I've also decided to cut back on those packaged snacks that I enjoyed eating so much. I think I've been eating way too much of them.

**Pam** But you are slim. I'm the one who should be watching what I'm eating. I think I've gained some weight recently. I'm having difficulty fitting myself into some of my clothes.

**Carol** But weight gain is just one of the problems. If you eat too much of those junk foods that are high in fat, salt and sugar, you are running the risk of developing health problems such as heart diseases and diabetes later on in life.

**Pam** That's frightening. I think I should cut back on my snack consumption too. But what should I do with this bag of potato chips? I've just opened it. Do you think I should throw it away?

**Carol** I have an idea. Let's share it and then go jogging for half an hour to burn off these extra calories that we take in.

**Pam** Sounds good. Let's dig in.

*Now make similar conversations of your own, using the given situations. Try to use in your conversations what you've learned in this lesson.*

**Situations:**

1) It's time for lunch now. Your roommate suggests a fast-food restaurant, but you would like something healthier.
2) One of your classmates complains to you about a health problem that she/he is suffering (for example, overweight, eating disorder, insomnia, depression, etc.). Try to find out what causes the problem and give suggestions as to what she/he needs to do to improve the situation.

# Part C Listen and Relax

## Epigrams

**Listen to the following five epigrams carefully and try to learn them by heart.**

| | |
|---|---|
| 1. *Diseases of the soul are more dangerous than those of the body.* 心灵的疾病比肉体的疾病更难医治。 | *— Cicero* |
| 2. *Prevention is better than cure.* 防病胜过治病。 | *— Charles Dickens* |
| 3. *Happiness lies, first of all, in health.* 幸福首先在于健康。 | *— G. W. Curtis* |
| 4. *Cheerfulness is the promoter of health.* 心情愉快是健康的增进剂。 | *— Joseph Addison* |
| 5. *Health is certainly more valuable than money, because it is by health that money is procured.* 健康当然比金钱更重要，因为健康带来金钱。 | *— Samuel Johnson* |

# Part D Further Listening

**A Passage**

## Organ Transplants

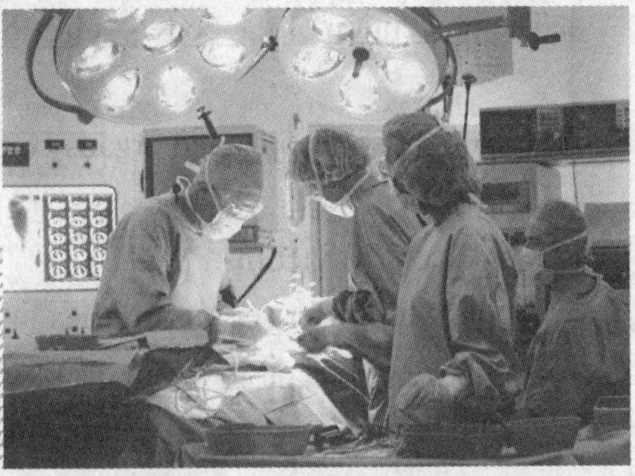

## Exercise

**You are going to hear a passage. Listen carefully and choose the right answer to each question you hear.**

Doctors around the world now can save thousands of lives with transplant operations. Each year, more than 20,000 organs are successfully transplanted into patients in the United States alone. These people can be expected to survive for many years.

At least 21 different organs and tissues can be successfully transplanted in the bodies of patients. The most common organ transplanted is a kidney. A scientific report on transplants said more than 24,000 kidney transplants are performed around the world each year. The success rate of these transplants is very high.

Tissue can also be transplanted. The most common tissue transplant is a blood transfusion when a patient receives blood after an operation or accident. Other tissues that are transplanted include corneas of the eye, skin, bone marrow, bone and blood vessels.

A transplant operation succeeds only if doctors can prevent the body from rejecting the foreign organ or tissue. This is done with drugs. The patient also must receive tissue that is similar to his or her own.

Family members are the best possible organ donors. Other healthy people also can provide organs. However, most transplanted organs come from people who died or are brain dead. People who are brain dead usually were in a serious accident that injured the head. After the brain dies, doctors keep the other part of the body alive with machines.

The family of the accident victim must give permission for transplanting the victim's organs. Then a local medical organization makes a computerized search for a person who needs the organ and who has the tissue similar to the victim. Doctors remove the organs from the body and send them to the recipient's hospital.

1. How many organs are successfully transplanted into patients each year in the U.S.?
   a. More than 24,000.
   b. More than 20,000.
   c. More than 21,000.
   d. More than 25,000.

2. What determines the success of a transplant operation?
   a. The physical condition of the patient.
   b. The physical condition of the donor.
   c. The kind of organ or tissue transplanted.
   d. The prevention of the body's rejection of the transplanted organs or tissues.

3. Where do most transplanted organs come from?
   a. Family members.
   b. Road accident victims.
   c. People who suffer serious injuries in accidents.
   d. People who died or are brain dead.

## A Conversation

# Bird Flu Outbreak in Hong Kong

### Exercise

**Listen to the conversation carefully and choose the right answer to each question you hear.**

**Interviewer** Dr Collins, does the bird flu virus affect people?

**Dr Collins** Bird flu usually does not affect people. However, sometimes the flu virus changes and it can change into a virus that kills people. In 1997, six people in Hong Kong died when they became infected with a flu virus found in chickens. Health officials then ordered the killing of all chickens, ducks and geese in Hong Kong.

**Interviewer** So far, what has been done to halt the spread of the virus?

**Dr Collins** This is the third time in five years that the bird flu virus has affected Hong Kong. Health workers are moving quickly before it can develop into a virus that kills people. They have already destroyed more than 150,000 chickens. They also have increased inspections of markets and farms where chickens are raised.

**Interviewer** How has the breakout of the virus this time affected the Hong Kong chicken markets?

**Dr Collins** Hong Kong has almost 7,000,000 people. Chicken is a popular food. People eat about 100,000 chickens every day. Traditionally, many people buy their chickens live from street markets and bring them home freshly killed. Hong Kong markets are still selling chickens, but sales have dropped sharply.

**Interviewer** What caused the breakout of the virus?

**Dr Collins** Some critics blame the problem on poor conditions at chicken farms. These include overcrowding, unclean conditions and lack of fresh air. I think these might be the root causes of the breakout of the virus.

**Interviewer** Thank you very much, Dr Collins.

1. Which of the following is true about bird flu?

   a. It poses no threat to people.

   b. <u>Its virus can change into another virus that kills poultry as well as people.</u>

   c. It's not an infectious disease.

   d. It's hard to cure the disease.

2. How many chickens have health workers in Hong Kong destroyed in the city's third outbreak of

bird flu?

a. Over 160,000.
b. Over 260,000.
c. Over 150,000.
d. Over 250,000.

3. What caused the breakout of the virus according to Dr Collins?
   a. Lack of knowledge on the part of citizens.
   b. Negligence on the part of health workers.
   c. Poor conditions at chicken farms.
   d. Dirty street markets.

# Part E Home Listening

## Passage 1

### Health Issues in Our Century

**Exercise**

**Listen to the passage about six most common causes of death in the world and fill in the chart with the missing information.**

What are the six most common causes of death in the world? Scientists have found that most people die from heart disease, cancer, AIDS, malaria, diarrhea, and road traffic accidents.

**Heart disease** can also be caused through bad diet and a lack of exercise. It can be prevented, and public awareness levels are high in some countries. However, some sections of the community seem to ignore advice. Treatment is possible but prevention is obviously preferable in the long term.

**Cancer** is caused by a number of factors. There is strong evidence that smoking and other lifestyle factors contribute significantly, especially to lung and throat cancers. Treatment can be through chemotherapy or radiotherapy, and success rates are increasing.

**AIDS** is preventable but, as yet, there is no known cure although there is treatment available. Research continues in the hope of finding out.

**Malaria** is a disease which is spread via mosquito bites. It is easily prevented with the use of mosquito repellents including electronic devices, creams and sprays. It can also be avoided by taking

pills regularly, which protect the body from the disease. Malaria cannot be cured as such, though its symptoms (headache, fever, and shaking) are treatable.

**Road traffic accidents** Road safety standards vary a lot from country to country. Drunk driving and the use of unsafe vehicles contribute to the deaths of hundreds of thousands of people around the world. Publicity campaigns and stricter laws have made a dramatic difference in some countries.

**Diarrhea** is one of the most common causes of death, especially among children, in Africa. It is caused by polluted water and a lack of food hygiene. It can be prevented by making water supplies safe. It is also important that public awareness is raised as to the causes of water contamination.

| Disease | Causes associated with the disease | Treatment and prevention |
|---|---|---|
| **Heart disease** | caused through 1) *bad diet* and a lack of 2) *exercise* | treatment 3) *possible*; prevention 4) *preferable* |
| **Cancer** | smoking and 5) *lifestyle factors* | through chemotherapy or radiotherapy |
| **AIDS** | not mentioned | It is 6) *preventable* but there is no known 7) *cure*. |
| **Malaria** | through mosquito bites | easily 8) *prevented*; can also be avoided by 9) *taking pills* regularly; cannot be 10) *cured* as such but its symptoms are 11) treatable |
| **Road traffic accidents** | 12) *drunk driving*; the use of 13) *unsafe vehicles* | 14) *stricter laws*; 15) *publicity campaigns* |
| **Diarrhea** | caused by 16) *polluted water* and a lack of 17) *food hygiene* | making 18) *water supplies* safe; raising 19) *public awareness* as to the cause of 20) *water contamination* |

**Passage 2**

# Valuable Tips in Hair Care

## Exercise

**Listen to the passage and choose the right answer to each question you hear.**

We change our hairstyle depending on what's in style. But what looks most flattering on our

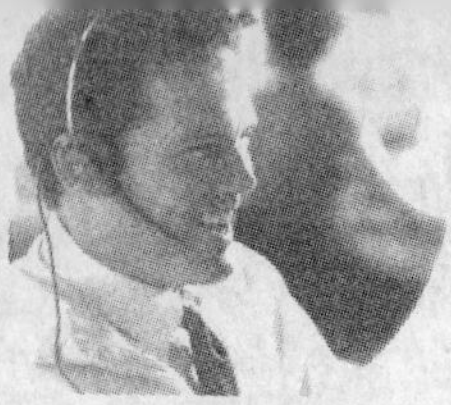



head is healthy hair, not necessarily stylish hair. There are a number of things we can do to keep our hair healthy and looking good.

An average person has 100,000 to 120,000 hairs on her head. Hair grows about 1 millimeter in three days, 12 – 15 centimeters over a year. The hair on top of our head grows at a faster rate than the hair on the sides. Hair growth goes through two stages, growing and falling out. It also differs seasonally. During fall and spring, hair tends to fall out more, while during summer it tends to grow faster. An average person loses about 100 hairs daily.

Emotional and physical stress, as well as environmental pollution, can cause our hair to fall out excessively. Diet lacking in protein and vitamins can also affect our hair. The hair can become brittle, lose its shine and fall out prematurely. Other factors that can contribute to excessive hair loss can be abusive hair treatments, such as constant exposure to the heat of a hair dryer, straightening iron, or curling device, as well as certain hairstyles, such as very tight ponytails. Similarly, chemical coloring, curling and straightening can cause hair to fall out.

In the summer, we should give our hair extra attention as excessive sun exposure makes our hair dryer and more brittle. Preferably, you should cover your hair with a hat or a scarf when spending time outside in the sun.

In order to keep our hair thick and healthy, we need to nourish it from inside. We need to have a diet that contains ample amounts of proteins, and consume good oils such as omega-3, vitamins A, E and B, as well as iron and zinc.

When picking hair products, look for shampoos containing substances that stimulate the roots of the hair to grow. While washing your hair, use a small amount of shampoo and work it in the palm of your hand to create a lather before applying it to your head. After washing, make sure to rinse thoroughly till all the dirt and chemicals are washed off. Afterwards, don't rub your wet hair with a towel, but rather squeeze out the water gently and comb through your hair with a wide-toothed comb. If using a hair dryer, use it on a cool setting. All of these tips can help you avoid damaging your fragile hair.

1. Which of the following is true about your hair?
   a. It grows slower on the top of your head than on the sides.
   b. It goes through two stages in its growth, growing and falling out.
   c. It falls out more during autumn and winter.
   d. It grows faster during spring.

2. What can cause your hair to fall out excessively?
   a. Washing your hair too often.
   b. Physical and emotional stress.
   c. Lacking in physical exercises.
   d. Diet lacking in Vitamins B and C.

3. What does the speaker advise you to do to keep your hair thick and healthy?
   a. Use shampoo and conditioner regularly to nourish your hair from outside.
   b. Use only a small amount of shampoo when washing your hair.
   c. Buy hair shampoos that contain ample amounts of protein.
   d. Have a diet that is rich in protein, vitamins and good oils.

4. After washing your hair, what is suggested that you do to avoid damaging it?
   a. Rub your hair with a towel.
   b. Comb your hair gently till it dries.
   c. Rinse thoroughly.
   d. Use a hair dryer on a hot setting.

5. Which of the following might the speaker be?
   a. A health worker.
   b. A hair care specialist.
   c. A hair stylist.
   d. A designer of hair products.

# Unit 5

# Viewpoint

## Part A Listening Activities

### A Passage

### Tipping

I'd be just as happy if they passed a law tomorrow making tipping illegal.

There are all sorts of things wrong with tipping. It puts both tipper and tippee in a bad position. Why should anyone have to depend on what I choose to give them for their services? Who am I to leave a dollar under my plate for the waiter as if I was doing him a big favor? I hate tipping.

The first thing wrong is that most of us don't know who to tip or how much. We don't know what the person we're tipping expects from us. We don't want him to think we're cheapskates, and we don't want to look as though we're from out of town by tipping too much. We just know we're supposed to do it.

I eat in a lot of restaurants during the course of a year, and the tip I leave the waiter or waitress very seldom bears any relationship to the quality of service I get. I leave the same tip for good service as I do for bad. Occasionally when service is really terrible, I'll shave the tip to the socially acceptable minimum but never below that. I'm a coward when it comes to tipping.

Years ago George Bernard Shaw ate in a restaurant in New York and the service was terrible. The waiter ignored him, got the orders mixed up and was rude. After the meal, Shaw paid the check and as he was leaving he looked the waiter in the eye and dropped a fifty-dollar bill on the table.

"This is what I tip for bad service," Shaw said.

The word "TIPS" is supposed to have come from the letters of the words "To Insure Prompt Service". I don't know whether that's true or not. All I know is it doesn't help the service at all and we ought to drop the custom.

There are a lot of small towns in the United States where no one would dream of tipping someone. That's the way it ought to be, but in the big cities you're expected to tip half the people you meet. In a hotel there are always a lot of people doing things for you that you'd rather do yourself, because they're looking for a tip. When there are nine taxicabs in a line outside the hotel, I don't need a doorman whistling his head off to get me one. I resent tipping doormen for doing almost nothing.

A friend of mine spent several days at the fancy Greenbrier Hotel in West Virginia once, and as he was leaving he held a dollar to a doorman who hadn't done anything for him and said, "Do you have some change?"

The doorman looked at my friend and said, "Sir, at the Greenbrier, a dollar is change."

Several times a year, I find myself in an expensive restaurant that has a washroom attendant. I'm perfectly capable of washing and drying my own hands without having an attendant hand me a towel, and I think the establishment should pay someone to keep the place neat and clean without making the clients pay for it with tips. The attendant usually has four or five dollar bills in a dish, as if that's what you're expected to leave.

I don't have my shoes shined anymore because it costs too much to tip. I've never known how much to give the captain in the restaurant with a washroom attendant and if I have to tip a headwaiter ten dollars for a good table, I'm going to eat some place else.

I'd like to put an end to all tipping, but I don't dare start the movement all by myself.

## New Words and Expressions

| | | | |
|---|---|---|---|
| tip | /tɪp/ | *v.* | 给小费 to give money to someone for service rendered |
| cheapskate | /ˈtʃiːpskeɪt/ | *n.* | 吝啬鬼 a person who is stingy and miserly |

coward /ˈkaʊəd/ *n.* 胆小鬼 a timid person

resent /rɪˈzent/ *v.* 怨恨 to feel bitterness or anger at something or someone

fancy /ˈfænsɪ/ *adj.* 高级且昂贵的 expensive and of superior grade

client /ˈklaɪənt/ *n.* 顾客 customer

shine /ʃaɪn/ *v.* 擦亮 to make (shoes, etc.) bright by rubbing

---

from out of town 来自外乡 from another town; not from a big city

come to 涉及 to be concerned with

look ... in the eye 正视某人 to look someone straight in the eye

(whistle /ˈwɪsl/) one's head off （口哨吹个）不停（以吸引某人注意） to blow whistles repeatedly in order to catch (someone's) attention

washroom attendant 盥洗室服务员 a person who cleans the washroom and waits on customers

## Language and Culture Notes

1. ***Background Information*** Tipping is a practice in the United States and many other countries in the world. It is a payment given to a waiter / waitress, a cab driver, a doorman, a porter, etc., besides the standard charge. In a restaurant, for example, waiters, busboys (young men whose jobs are to take away dirty dishes), etc., are paid very low wages and they depend on the tips they receive from diners to support themselves. The socially acceptable standard of a tip to a waiter is about 15% of the charge of one's meal. In other words, if the meal costs $30, the diner is expected to leave another $4.5 or more on the table as the tip. In other situations, it is often quite puzzling as to how much one should spend on tipping, especially when one feels that the service is bad or unnecessary.
2. ***George Bernard Shaw*** (1856–1950) Irish-born playwright, whose major works include *Arms and Man*, *Man and Superman*, *Major Barbara*, *Pygmalion and St. Joan*. He won Nobel Prize for literature in 1925.

3. ***one's head off*** (*slang*) loudly or excessively
4. ***washroom attendant*** one whose job is to keep the washroom clean and render services (such as handing over the towel, or even wiping the toilet seat after each use) to people. Such attendants are found only in expensive hotels and they expect to be tipped for their services.
5. ***captain*** (U.S.) a headwaiter

## Exercise 1

**Listen to the passage and then choose the right answer to each question you hear.**

1. What is the speaker's attitude toward tipping?
   a. He thinks it is socially acceptable in big cities.
   b. He thinks it is an employer's job to tip his employees handsomely.
   c. He thinks it is terrible to give away money in such a wasteful way.
   d. He thinks it puts both parties involved in an awkward situation.

2. Why do most people tip the service people, such as waiters and hotel attendants, according to the speaker?
   a. They are mostly grateful for the services they have received.
   b. They know the service people are poorly paid and depend on them for their living.
   c. They are compelled to do it because they know that is what they are expected to do.
   d. They are afraid to offend the people who have provided them with services.

3. What can you learn from the text about the speaker?
   a. He dines more in restaurants than at home.
   b. He usually leaves the same amount of money for a tip regardless of the quality of the service.
   c. He is from a small town and doesn't know how to tip appropriately.
   d. He sometimes leaves no tip for a bad service.

4. What conclusions can NOT be drawn about the doorman at the Greenbrier Hotel?
   a. He is snobbish and conceited.
   b. He is used to big tips.
   c. He regards one dollar as insignificant as small change.
   d. He would feel ashamed to receive a tip for doing nothing.

5. What is the speaker's tone?
   a. Ironic.
   b. Humorous.
   c. Pessimistic.
   d. Helpless.

### Exercise 2

**Listen to the recording again and as you listen, jot down brief notes to help you answer the following questions.**

1. What are most people's fears when it comes to tipping?
   a. *They don't know who to tip or how much*.
   b. *They don't know what the person they're tipping expects from them*.
   c. *They don't want the tippee to think they're cheapskates and they don't want to look as though they're from out of town by tipping too much*.
2. What kind of service did Bernard Shaw once receive from a waiter in a New York restaurant? What did the waiter do? What was Shaw's reaction?
   *Bernard Shaw received a terrible service. The waiter ignored the great playwright and mixed up his orders. On top of all this, he was rude. After paying the check Shaw looked the waiter in the eye, dropped a fifty-dollar bill on the table and said, "This is what I tip for bad service."*
3. What is the word "TIPS" supposed to stand for?
   *To Insure Prompt Service*.
4. In the washroom episode, how much money did the attendant probably expect people to leave in the dish?
   *One dollar*.

## Part B Speaking Activities

### Pair Work

### Exercise 1

**Listen to the recording again and discuss the following questions in class.**

1. What do you think of tipping? Do you agree with the speaker that it puts both the tipper and tippee in a bad position? Why?

2. What solutions are suggested, seriously and humorously, in the text to end tipping? What is your advice to the speaker?
(Employers should pay their employees a decent wage instead of letting them depend on tips from clients for their living; follow the practice of many small towns and stop tipping. [suggested seriously]
To pass a law making tipping illegal. [suggested just for fun])
3. Why did Bernard Shaw tip the rude waiter so handsomely?
(Probably to make him feel ashamed of his behavior.)

## Exercise 2

**While tipping is not common in China, it is usually practiced in many English speaking countries where you are expected to pay a small sum of money to cab drivers, porters, and to service people at restaurants and hotels. Tipping practices vary from region to region and from country to country. Provided below is a rough guide about tipping in the United States. Read the information in the table and think about how you would advise foreign visitors about tipping in China.**

| **Tipping Etiquette in the USA** | |
|---|---|
| **Rule of thumb** | Tipping is widely practiced in the United States. Customers are expected to tip when receiving a service. |
| **To whom?** | Waiters and waitresses in restaurants (tipping is not expected in fast food restaurants where nobody waits on your table), hotel staff, airport porters, cab drivers, tourist guides and drivers, etc. |
| **How much?** | Waiters and waitresses: 10%–20% of the bill, depending on the level of service received. 15% for average service, 20% for exceptionally good service, and 10% for mediocre service. For terrible service, lower than 10% or none.<br>Hotel and airport porters: $1 per piece of luggage (normal size). For heavier items, $2 per piece.<br>Cab drivers: 10% of fare. Add $1 per bag placed in trunk. |
| **Why tip?** | a. Reward for good service.<br>b. Employees in service areas are usually paid low wages as they are supposed to be compensated by tips. Americans understand this situation and generally tip unless the service is terrible. |

| | |
|---|---|
| **Other information** | a. There's no law that says you have to tip. It's still up to the customer to decide whether to tip or not.<br>b. While customers are expected to tip, it's considered extremely rude and inappropriate for a service worker to directly ask a customer for a tip. |

*Now work in pairs and make a dialogue based on the given situation:*

**Situation:** An American exchange student in China is having a meal with one of his/her Chinese friends. The topic of tipping crops up in the conversation. They explain to each other the tipping customs in their own countries and inquire about what the customs are in the other's country.

# Part C Listen and Relax

## Tongue Twisters

**Listen to the following tongue twisters and repeat them after the recording. Try to say them as quickly and correctly as possible.**

(1)

*There is a kitten in my kitchen;*
*in the kitchen I fry the chicken.*
*A fly flies into the kitchen,*
*while I fry the chicken.*

(2)

*Betty bought a bit of butter.*
*"But," she said, "this butter's bitter.*
*If I put it in my batter,*
*It will make my batter bitter.*
*But a bit of better butter —*
*That would make my batter better."*
*So Betty bought a bit of better butter,*

*And she put it in her bitter batter,*
*And made her bitter batter a bit better.*

# Part D Further Listening

## A Conversation

### What Do You Think of the Service of the Restaurant?

**Exercise**

**Listen to the conversation and write down your answers to the questions given in the opinion form.**

You are the manager of Gourmet Restaurant. You want to conduct a survey of your customers' opinions on how to improve the service of the restaurant. You interview one of the customers and record his opinions. Here is the interview with the customer.

**M** Excuse me, we would like to improve our service and would like to know what you think about our restaurant. Could you spare me some time?
**W** By all means.
**M** How often do you come to our restaurant every month?
**W** 3 to 5 times, I think.
**M** How did you know of our restaurant?
**W** Well, some friends of mine recommend your restaurant to me.
**M** Do you usually come here for lunch or dinner?
**W** I usually come here for dinner.
**M** What is your favorite food in our restaurant?
**W** Uh, let me see. There are several dishes which I like a lot, such as curry chicken, lamb chop and fish fillet. They are delicious indeed. I order them quite often.

**M** Thank you for your appreciation. What about the quality of food in general?

**W** On the whole, it is not bad. But I still have a complaint to make. That is, the food is usually too greasy. Perhaps, it would be better to use less oil for food.

**M** Are there any items of food that you think should be added to our menu?

**W** Actually, I like to eat vegetarian food. I think you would attract more vegetarian customers if you offer more vegetarian dishes.

**M** Mmm. Very interesting. I've written down your opinions and they are valuable indeed. Thanks a lot.

**W** You are welcome.

**Gourmet Restaurant Customer Opinion Form**

1. How often do you come to the restaurant every month?
   *3 to 5 times*.
2. How did you learn about our restaurant?
   *My friends recommended the restaurant to me*.
3. What is / are your favorite dish(es)?
   *Curry chicken, lamb chop and fish fillet*.
4. What do you think of the quality of the food?
   *On the whole, it's not bad. But it is usually too greasy*.
5. What dishes should be added to the menu?
   *Vegetarian dishes*.

## A Compound Dictation

### Exercise

**Listen to the passage three times and supply the missing information.**

Both e-mail and the cell phone are 1) *amazing* inventions in the late 20th century that have contributed greatly to the 2) *ease* of communication within and across nations. It would be hard to decide which of the two has been more 3) *beneficial* to mankind. Like e-mail communication, the cell phone has contributed greatly to an 4) *enormous* increase in the volume and 5) *efficiency* of business deals. Similarly the cell phone has been just as 6) *crucial* as e-mail communication in helping family and friends to keep in touch even when they live apart. The cost of using a cell phone is similar to that of using e-mail. Both are quite expensive

but for different reasons. With e-mail, it is the 7) *initial* investment of buying a computer that is expensive; with cell phones, the cost can be quite high. Despite the similarity between the two, there are also some major differences. In the first place, cell phone communication is a lot more convenient than e-mail communication. 8) *You can carry a cell phone with you wherever you go; you can't do this with your PC*. On some cell phones, you can access your e-mail, but that is not the same as having full e-mail and Internet facilities on your PC. 9) *Unlike e-mail communication, cell phone communication allows for a wide range of human emotions*. The person you're talking to can tell from your voice if you are sad, angry and happy. Closely related to this is the fact that with cell phone communication, you know — again because of the voice — who might be dangerous in some way. 10) *Whereas, however, health hazards are not so likely with e-mail, with the cell phone, there appears to be a real risk that excessive use may result in the development of brain tumors.*

# Part E Home Listening

## Forum 1

### Welcome to the Show "On the Street"

#### Exercise

**Listen to the show "On the Street" carefully and complete the answers to the questions given below.**

**Announcer** Welcome to the show "On the Street", the show that always asks the most interesting questions. We're here on Republic Avenue this time, and today's question is: Should our country host the next World Cup finals? Hi, what's your name?

**Gina** Gina.

**Announcer** And what do you think, Gina? Should our country host the next World Cup finals?

**Gina** [*laughing*] Well, you know, our country isn't very big and a lot of foreigners can't even find it on a map. I know, because I was an exchange student in the U.S. last year,

and when I told people where I was from, they always said, "Where's that?" So if we have the World Cup here, we'll get lots of overseas visitors and other people will at least see it on TV, so they might get to know a little more about our culture and our country. So I think it would be a good thing, all in all.

**Announcer** Thanks, Gina. Let's get another point of view, from this young man. Will you give us your name, please?

**Lee** Hi, my name is Lee.

**Announcer** And what's your opinion, Lee — should our country host the World Cup?

**Lee** [*somewhat irritable*] Can you imagine how much that would cost? We have only one good-sized stadium in the whole country, so we'd have to build at least four or five more. And then we'd have to have a bigger airport to handle all the visitors, and we'd need better highways for them to drive around on. There are so many other more important things to spend that money on. We should just forget about this whole World Cup idea.

**Announcer** Thanks for talking with us, Lee. We have time for one more opinion. What's your name?

**Anita** Anita.

**Announcer** Tell us, Anita, do you think our country should host the World Cup?

**Anita** [*bubbly*] I think it would be a fantastic opportunity, I mean, everyone here is just crazy about soccer. Kids play it, adults play it — we'd all have a chance to watch some of the biggest names in soccer, playing right here. And I think seeing them would encourage kids to play more seriously, and over time, I think it will raise the standard of sports here. I mean, there's no way we'll win the World Cup any time soon, but we can at least see the winners.

**Announcer** Thank you, Anita, and thanks to all of you for being with us today.

1. What's the topic of the show?
   Should our country *host the next World Cup finals*?
2. What does the first speaker Gina think of it? Why?
   She says it would be *a good thing* because it will make their country, which is not very big, known to people in the world. Lots of *overseas visitors will come* and those who do not come will at least *see it on TV*.
3. What's the second speaker's opinion?
   He thinks it's *too costly to host the game*. They'll have to build stadiums, a bigger airport, and better highways to handle *the game and the visitors*. He thinks *the money should be spent on many other important things*. He suggests they should just *forget about this whole World Cup idea*.
4. What does the last speaker Anita think of the idea?
   She thinks it would be *a fantastic opportunity*. People, kids as well as adults, are *crazy about*

*soccer* and they will have a chance *to watch some of the biggest names* in soccer, playing right in their country. And seeing great soccer players would *encourage kids to play more seriously*, and over time, it will *raise the standard of sports in the country*.

**Forum 2**

## Aren't Children Affected by TV Violence?

### Exercise

**You're going to hear part of a radio phone-in program. Listen carefully and decide whether the opinions given below are expressed in the calls. Put a tick in the brackets.**

**Presenter** A recent survey revealed that in one week on British TV 401 people were killed and 119 were wounded. Similar research in the US showed that the average American child watches 8,000 murders and 100,000 other acts of violence while still at junior school. What effect has this been having on our children? So do you agree that what children see on TV affects their behavior? Should we have stricter controls on what can or can't be shown? Or should people be able to watch anything that they want? We'd like to hear your views, so please call us. … Here's our first caller. What would you like to say?

**Middle-aged woman** Well, I just can't believe it when people say that children aren't affected by TV violence. Of course they are. We all know that children love to act out things that they have seen in films and so on. Now that's all right if they're acting out a scene from *Cinderella*, but if they can act out things like that, they can act out violent things, can't they? It's obvious.

**Presenter** Thank you for that and now our next caller.

**Middle-aged man** I agree with what the last speaker said, but any TV has got a switch on it. If you don't want your children to watch something, switch it off. In my opinion, it's the parents' responsibility to make sure that kids haven't been watching unsuitable things. I should be able to watch what I want. It's not my problem.

**Presenter** What does our next speaker think about that?

**Young mother** I'm sorry, but I can't agree. I mean, he says it's not his problem, but it is his problem if he gets attacked by a teenager who's been watching violent movies. If we breed a violent society, we all suffer. I try to control what my children watch but it isn't easy. They can always go round to their friends' houses and watch videos.

**Presenter** Thank you. Now what does our next caller want to say?

**Young man** I simply don't agree with the results of the research. How can we prove that when somebody acts violently it's because they've been watching TV programs? You know, millions of people watch violent films but they don't all become murderers, do they? We can't blame television for everything that's wrong with society. I maintain it's just an excuse for censorship.

**Presenter** Well, we've certainly got a wide range of views. Now let's take a break for some music. Then we'll put those views to our experts in the studio …

1. Children love to act out things that they have seen in films. ( √ )
2. Children like to act out violent things more than scenes from *Cinderella*. ( )
3. Children are not affected by TV violence. ( )
4. Parents should be responsible for their children's behavior. ( )
5. Parents should make sure that their children do not watch unsuitable programs. ( √ )
6. It's hard for parents to control what their children watch. ( √ )
7. Adults should be allowed to watch anything they want. ( √ )
8. There is too much bad language on TV. ( )
9. It's unfair to blame violent TV programs for things that go wrong in society. ( √ )
10. It's an excuse to ban certain TV programs. ( √ )

# Unit 6

# Culture

## Part A Listening Activities

### A Forum

#### Why Go Abroad?

**Matthew** Lesley, why do most people go abroad?

**Lesley** It depends. For some, of course, it's business; for those who concentrate more on pleasure, it's just getting away from wherever they happen to be.

**Matthew** Michael, do you travel a lot?

**Michael** A reasonable amount. Obviously one ... would like to travel all the time, to see er ... other countries and other places and other people, and to see the fascinating things that are so different from one country to another. There are enormous difficulties put in our ways of traveling by things like er ... having passports to gain access from country to

country, the difficulties of er ... changing money from one currency to another currency, the difficulties of language of course, er ... are preeminent.

**Matthew** Maggie ... do you think it's important that people travel?

**Maggie** Mm, yes, I think it's very important. It broadens your mind and by traveling ... abroad you find that you can pick up their languages and that you can communicate with other people, and it ... it helps a lot to meet foreigners.

**Matthew** But young people often don't have the sort of money to get on a luxury cruise liner or a fast jet somewhere. How can young people travel reasonably economically?

**Maggie** Well, if you're a student, or if you're u ... under twenty-one there are special ... concessions that the airlines have. Or you can get a ... a special stu ... student flight, student ... trains to travel abroad, or quite a lot of young people on their first trip abroad um ... travel by hitch-hiking. It ... it's a method which I have used myself but ... er ... I wouldn't advise it to anybody; it ... it helps if you speak the language of the country that you're in, but it is one ... one way of seeing different parts of the world and ... and fairly cheaply.

**Matthew** Are there any big problems in traveling from country to country, er ... for the young person today?

**Maggie** Well, I think probably if you don't speak the language and you land in a ... in a town ... abroad and you haven't got friends in the place, then it probably is quite difficult ... um, but so many places now are used to having young people as tourists, that they ... they help you in the streets, they help you to find places, but ... but I think the language is the most important.

**Matthew** Alan, you've not only traveled widely but you now live abroad. What problems are there for somebody who wants to go and live and work in a foreign country?

**Alan** Work permits are usually a problem; in every country I've been in they've been a problem, um ... residence visas are a problem um ... getting people to understand what you want in er ... in so far as bureaucrats are concerned is a ... is a very great problem um ... However, the first time is the worst, and after that you begin to realise the way these people er ... er think and act, and in fact they're not so um ... so troublesome, as at first you think they are. In fact, they're trying to help you but er ... perhaps in a rather obscure and oblique way.

**Matthew** What's the advantage of living in a country as opposed to just visiting it briefly?

**Alan** Well, if you visit a country briefly then you're really just a tourist, and if you're a tourist you will find that you'll be um ... side-tracked into er ... hotels which will, in fact, just be like living at er ... home. You'll probably be fed English food, etcetera and you'll be with um ... your own er ... people. If you actually live abroad you'll find that um ... you actually get into contact with the people, and the language of the country where you're living, and er … you'll learn a new way of life and you'll learn to understand a new way of life and this should, but not always, er ... give you an insight into

your own way of life, the way of life you led in England. Well, whether this is a good thing or a bad thing I can't tell you, but er ... it's led me to be able to er ... differentiate between um ... cultures and ways of living um ... I've lived in two countries, myself, in three countries in fact. At first when I went to these countries I ... I thought, well, perhaps my way of living is better; then afterwards I thought perhaps their way of living is better. Now I just realise they're different.

## New Words and Expressions

| | | | |
|---|---|---|---|
| access | /ˈækses/ | *n.* | 进入权 permission to enter |
| currency | /ˈkʌrənsɪ/ | *n.* | 货币 a system of money in general use in a particular country |
| preeminent | /ˌpriːˈemɪnənt/ | *adj.* | 首要的 more important than all others |
| concession | /kənˈseʃən/ | *n.* | 让步 the thing or point yielded |
| bureaucrat | /ˈbjʊərəʊkræt/ | *n.* | 官僚主义者 an official of a bureaucracy who works by rigid routine |
| obscure | /əbˈskjʊə/ | *adj.* | 意思含糊的 unclear and difficult to understand or see |
| oblique | /əˈbliːk/ | *adj.* | 转弯抹角的 indirectly expressed |
| insight | /ˈɪnsaɪt/ | *n.* | 深入了解 an instance of understanding the true nature of something |
| differentiate | /ˌdɪfəˈrenʃɪeɪt/ | *v.* | 区别 to distinguish |
| work permit | | | 打工许可证 employment authorization document |
| residence visa | | | 居住签证 an official document that permits a foreigner to live in another country |
| as opposed to ... | | | 与……相对的 in contrast with |
| be side-tracked into ... | | | 使偏离至…… to be directed away from an activity or subject toward another one (that is often less important) |
| pick up (their languages) | | | （未经正规学习）学会（语言） to learn (their languages without formal study) |
| Lesley | /ˈlezlɪ/ | | （女子名） name *(f.)* |

## Language and Culture Notes

1. ***Background Information*** The urge to travel abroad is very strong in the hearts of many people in the world. Although a large number of them travel on business, many people go abroad as tourists. They want to see different places and learn about different cultures. International tourism has promoted friendship between peoples of different races and nations.
2. ***special concessions that the airlines have*** airlines make special concessions to those who are under 21 and offer them tickets at reduced prices

## Exercise 1

**Listen to the discussion and choose the right answer to each question you hear.**

1. Why do some people travel abroad according to Lesley?
   a. They go abroad on business or for pleasure.
   b. They go abroad for study or for pleasure.
   c. They go abroad for a better job and a better living.
   d. They get bored of life at home and they go abroad for a change.

2. What is Maggie's attitude towards hitch-hiking?
   a. Positive. b. Negative.
   c. Doubtful. d. Appreciative.

3. What two big problems do young people have while traveling according to Maggie?
   a. They are often lost in a new place and they can't get help from anybody.
   b. They don't speak the language and they have no acquaintances there.
   c. They don't have enough money and they can hardly find a cheap hotel.
   d. They can hardly get used to the way of living there and they have to deal with bureaucrats.

4. What seems to be one of the advantages of living in a foreign country according to Alan?
   a. You'll learn to appreciate your own culture.
   b. You'll learn to accept different cultures and different ways of life.
   c. You'll feel like living at home.
   d. You'll learn a better way of living.

5. Which of the following can be learned from the conversation?
   a. Living in a foreign country is better than staying merely as a tourist.

b. Once the language barrier is overcome, people will have no problem in a foreign country.

<u>c. Young students can travel abroad fairly cheaply.</u>

d. It's easier for young people to travel abroad than old people.

## Exercise 2

**You are going to hear some parts of the discussion again. Each part will be read twice. After each part you will be asked a question. Listen carefully and write down your answer in the blank.**

1. "There are enormous difficulties put in our ways of traveling by things like er ... having passports to gain access from country to country, the difficulties of er ... changing money from one currency to another currency, and the difficulties of language of course, er ... are preeminent."

   **Question:** What are the difficulties mentioned in this part?

   *<u>Getting passports, changing money from one currency to another currency, and learning to speak foreign languages.</u>*

2. "Mm, yes, I think it's very important. It broadens your mind and by traveling ... abroad you find that you can pick up their languages and that you can communicate with other people, and it ... it helps a lot to meet foreigners."

   **Question:** What are the advantages of going abroad?

   *<u>Broadening one's mind, picking up foreign languages and communicating with local people.</u>*

3. "Alan, you've not only traveled widely but you now live abroad. What problems are there for somebody who wants to go and live and work in a foreign country?".

   "Work permits are usually a problem; in every country I've been in they've been a problem, um ... residence visas are a problem um ... getting people to understand what you want in er ... in so far as bureaucrats are concerned is a ... is a very great problem um ..."

   **Question:** What problems would you have if you want to live and work in a foreign country?

   *<u>Obtaining work permits, residence visas and getting bureaucrats to understand what you want.</u>*

4. "However, the first time is the worst, and after that you begin to realise the way these people er ... er think and act, and in fact they're not so um ... so troublesome, as at first you think they are. In fact, they're trying to help you but er ... perhaps in a rather obscure and oblique way."

   **Question:** After Alan has settled down in a new place for some time, what does he think of the people who seemed to him so troublesome at first?

   *<u>Helpful, but not in a straightforward way.</u>*

# Part B Speaking Activities

## 1. Pair Work

*Answer the following questions orally. You may use the information you've got from the text or from your own experience.*

1) What places have you traveled to?
2) How did you enjoy your trips? Did you have any problems during your trips?
3) How can you travel fairly cheaply in China?
4) What difficulties do you think an immigrant may have when he or she first comes to settle down in a new place?
(Language barrier, a new way of living, residence visas, work permits, race prejudices, unfamiliar surroundings, few or no friends, homesickness, etc.)

## 2. Communicative Function: Understanding Cultural Differences

Culture is the way of life of a particular group of people. It includes everything from language, art, religion and customs to the clothes people wear, the food they eat and the holidays they observe. Different groups of people have different cultures. What is acceptable in one culture may be frowned upon in another. The same gesture may have totally different meanings in different countries. Cultural differences are often a cause of confusion, embarrassment, and even conflicts in cross-cultural communication. Have you ever felt surprised, confused or embarrassed by the actions of someone from another culture? How important do you think it is to learn about other cultures? How can we deal with cultural differences? In the box below, there are some sentences and structures that you may find useful when talking about cultural differences.

## UNDERSTANDING CULTURAL DIFFERENCES

Culture has to do with values and beliefs / involves customs and traditions.

In addition to language differences, different cultures have different beliefs, traditions, customs and observe different holidays.

There are cultural differences between different regions within the same country.

Culture influences and shapes our values and behavior / the way we see the world and ourselves / what we do, think and feel.

Culture awareness is often unconscious. People are sometimes not aware of how their behaviors and attitudes have been shaped by their culture.

People from different cultures differ in the way they want others to view and treat them / in how much they guard their privacy ...

Different cultures have different ways of greeting each other / responding to compliments / doing business / showing respect / expressing love and affection ...

Sometimes cultural differences are subtle and may go unrecognized / overlooked.

Failure to recognize / Lack of awareness of cultural differences can lead to misunderstanding / make communication difficult.

We tend to judge other cultures in terms of the values and customs of our own culture.

We tend to be condescending or even hostile toward other cultures.

All nations have stereotyped images of other nations.

Misleading stereotypes and prejudices can prevent us from understanding and appreciating another culture.

We should avoid a right versus wrong attitude toward cultural differences.

The more we learn about other cultures, the less likely are we to judge other people unfairly.

When in foreign countries, we should follow / heed the advice: "When in Rome, do as the Romans do."

Having respect for / Learning about other cultures can help you avoid misunderstandings / embarrassing situations / giving unintended offenses.

Understanding can only be reached if we are willing to treat people from other cultures with respect and as equals.

It's easy to make mistakes in etiquette when we are in foreign countries, but as long as we are respectful and show a willingness to understand and adapt to local customs, people are usually forgiving.

Cultural diversity is what makes the world so rich and so colorful.
Learning about other cultures makes you more aware of your own culture / opens your eyes to new ways of looking at the world around us.
No matter where they live, people throughout the world are similar in that they all have the same basic needs such as food, clothing, shelter, companionship and so on.
Regardless of cultural differences, there are universal values that we all agree on.
All cultures are fundamentally alike no matter how different they may seem from the outside.

## A Model

**An Interview**

*(Mark is interviewing a classmate, Shane, about cultural differences.)*

**Mark** Shane, have you ever visited a foreign country?

**Shane** Yes, I went to Thailand last summer with my parents.

**Mark** Are there any local customs in Thailand that struck you as interesting or strange?

**Shane** Sure. One thing I found interesting is how the Thai people attach different levels of importance to different parts of the body. For example, the head is considered the most sacred part of the body, so you are not supposed to touch anyone's head in Thailand. On the contrary, the feet are considered the lowest and dirtiest part, so you have to be careful not to point them at another person or use them to move things. Then the right hand is considered clean and the left hand unclean. You should use your right hand to eat food and never use the left hand to shake hands or receive gifts.

**Mark** That's interesting. Different cultures have different customs and rules of behavior. Do you think cultural differences can be a source of problems in cross-cultural communication?

**Shane** Yes, I think so. I think we are so used to the ways we do things in our own culture that we tend to take them for granted. We think they are "normal" or "natural" and expect people from other cultures to behave as we do. But the fact is they don't. What are good manners in one culture may be bad manners in another. If you are ignorant of such cultural differences, problems will surely arise. For example, in our country, it's normal to pat a child's head to show affection, but if you go to Thailand and pat a child's head to show your affection, you'll offend the child's parents without even knowing why.

**Mark** But how can we deal with cultural differences?

**Shane** I think we must first of all learn about other cultures so as to avoid causing unnecessary

offense or misunderstanding. But more importantly, I think we should always treat people from other cultures with respect. We tend to view people who are different from us as odd or even inferior, but we have to remember that all cultures are equal. In fact, if we are willing to put down our prejudices and try to see things from other people's perspectives, we'll discover that they are not as different from us as they may seem. After all, we are all human beings.

**Mark** Sure. Thank you, Shane. I do appreciate your insights.

**Shane** My pleasure.

*Now use the above interview as an example and interview some of your classmates about their thoughts on cultural differences. The following are some more questions you may want to use for the interview.*

1) Name the things that define culture.
2) How do you acquire your own culture?
3) What are some of the stereotypes that people from other countries have about Chinese people? Do you think they are fair or unfair?
4) How important do you think it is to respect local customs when you are in another region or another country?
5) Would you ever consider marrying or dating someone from another culture?
6) A famous writer on culture once said: "Cultural differences are a nuisance at best and often a disaster." Do you agree?

## Part C Listen and Relax

### A Poem

**Here is a short poem written by the English poet Charlotte Gray (1937– ). Listen and read along.**

#### *What Do I Wish You?*

*The family reunited, all squabbles set aside,*

*Food in the larder, knocks at the door,*
*Friendly faces, parcels piling up,*
*Cards from everyone you love,*
*Hugs, kisses, happy memories.*
*I wish with all my heart that*
*Your Christmas will be all that it was meant to be —*
*A little warmth in the depth of winter, a light in the dark.*

**Notes**

1. ***all squabbles set aside*** 把一切争吵搁置一边。
2. ***larder*** 食品室

# Part D Further Listening

## A Compound Dictation

### Exercise

**Listen to the passage three times and supply the missing information.**

American visitors to East Asia are often surprised and 1) *puzzled* by how Asian culture and customs differ from those in the United States. What's considered typical or proper social 2) *conduct* in one country may be regarded as 3) *odd*, improper or even rude in the other. For example, people from some East Asian countries may begin a conversation with a stranger by asking personal questions about family, home or work. Such questions are thought to be friendly 4) *whereas* they might be considered 5) *offensive* in the United States. On the other hand people in most Asian cultures are far more 6) *guarded* about expressing their feelings publicly than most Americans are. Openly displaying anger, 7) *yelling*, arguing loudly is considered bad-mannered in countries such as Japan.

8) *Many East Asians prefer to hold their emotions in check and instead express*

<u>*themselves with great politeness.*</u> They try not to be blunt and avoid making direct criticisms. In fact, 9) <u>*they often keep their differences of opinion to themselves and merely smile and remain silent rather than engage in an argument.*</u> By comparison, Americans are often frank about displaying both positive and negative emotions on the street and in other public places. Americans visiting Asia should keep in mind that such behavior may cause offense. 10) <u>*A major difference between American culture and most East Asian cultures is that in East Asia the community is more important than the individual.*</u> But in the United States, if you can make a name for yourself, you are considered a success.

## A Passage

# A World Guide to Good Manners

### Exercise

**Listen to the passage and make brief notes to help you complete the answers to the questions you hear.**

Traveling to all corners of the world gets easier and easier. We live in a global village, but how well do we know and understand each other? Here is a simple test. Imagine you have arranged a meeting at 4 o'clock, what time should you expect your foreign business colleagues to arrive? If they're German, they'll be right on time. If they're American, they'll be 15 minutes early. If they're British, they'll be 15 minutes late, and you should allow up to an hour for the Italians.

When the European Community began to increase in size, several guidebooks appeared giving advice on international etiquette. At first many people thought this was a joke, especially the British, who seemed to assume that the widespread understanding of their language meant a corresponding understanding of English customs. Very soon they had to change their ideas, as they realized that they had a lot to learn about how to behave with their foreign business friends.

For example: the British are happy to have a business lunch and discuss business matters with a drink during the meal; the Japanese prefer not to work while eating. To them lunch is a time to relax and get to know one another and they rarely drink at lunchtime. The Germans like to talk business before dinner; the French like to eat first and talk afterwards. They have to be well fed and watered before they discuss anything. Taking off your jacket and rolling up your sleeves is a sign of getting down to work in Britain and Holland, but in Germany people regard it as taking it easy.

1. What time should you expect your foreign business colleagues to arrive according to the passage?

   The Germans *on time*

   The Americans *15 minutes early*

   The British *15 minutes late*

   The Italians *at least an hour late*

2. What should you expect your foreign business friends to behave when it comes to discuss business matters over a meal?

   The British are happy to have a business lunch and *discuss business matters with a drink during the meal*.

   The Japanese prefer *not to work while eating and they seldom drink at lunchtime*.

   The Germans like to *talk business before dinner*.

   The French like to *eat first and talk afterward*.

# Part E Home Listening

## Passage 1

### Marriage Customs

#### Exercise

**Listen to the passage and choose the right answer to each question you hear.**

Despite the recent growth in the number of divorces, we in the West still tend to regard courtship and marriage as a romantic business. Boy meets girl, boy falls in love with girl, boy asks girl to marry him, girl accepts. Wedding, flowers, big celebration.

But in other parts of the world things work differently. In India, for instance, arranged marriage is still very common. Young couple meet for the first time on the day of the wedding. In Japan, too, arranged marriages still take place. The boy and the girl are introduced. They get a chance to have a look at one another. If one of them says, "Oh, no, I could never marry him or her," they call the whole thing off. But if they like one another, then the wedding goes ahead.

In parts of Africa, a man is allowed to have several wives. That sounds fine from the man's point of view, but in fact the man is taking on a great responsibility. When he takes a new wife and

buys her a nice present, he has to buy all his other wives presents at equal value and, the wives often become very close and so, if there is disagreement in the family, the husband has three or four wives to argue with instead of just one.

Most Westerners will assume that the Western style of marriage is the one with the greatest chance of producing a happy marriage. Marriage must always be something of a gambling. My observations have led me to believe that various forms of arranged marriage have just as much chance of bringing happiness to the husband and wife as our Western system of choosing marriage partners.

1. Where do young couples meet for the first time on the wedding day?
   a. In some Western countries.
   b. In India.
   c. In Japan.
   d. In some African countries.

2. Which of the following is true of an African man who has several wives?
   a. He must buy as many presents as possible to his wives.
   b. He may get himself in big trouble.
   c. He has to take on a great responsibility.
   d. He often has to argue with his wives.

3. What does the speaker believe in terms of an arranged marriage?
   a. It is very likely to leave the couple very miserable.
   b. It may also bring happiness to the couple.
   c. It is out of fashion.
   d. It should be abandoned.

**Passage 2**

## More Than a Bookstore

### Exercise

**Listen to the passage and choose the right answer to each question you hear.**

Symposia is a secondhand bookstore. But to my mind it is more than that. It's a community

meeting place. Owned and operated by Cornel and Carmen Rusu, it has the kind of atmosphere that makes you feel immediately at home. You're free to browse the stacks or talk with the owners about the programs they offer. Carmen manages the bookstore, while Cornel oversees the programs.

"We have a weekly conversation group called the Salon that started meeting shortly after Sept. 11," said Cornel, who is a social worker.

The diverse group, who range in age from early 20s to senior citizens and come from all ethnic backgrounds, get together on Wednesday nights from 7 to 9 in the evening to discuss everything from politics to sexuality. No subject is taboo. The weekly topic, chosen by the group, is introduced in advance on Symposia's website. Refreshments are served and all are welcome. "It's an open environment for people to share ideas and learn other perspectives," Cornel said.

There are two puppet shows for toddlers every weekday and Sunday. Symposia presents two new shows a week. The cost is $12 and includes a class afterwards with playtime, songs and crafts. Symposia also features monthly art shows. There are textual paintings, shadow puppets and ceramics, along with some very sophisticated examples of art drawn from other cultures.

The bookstore also has a poetry reading on the first Sunday of the month, a monthly book club, which meets on the fourth Thursday, and a movie night. Charitable organizations can contact Symposia and they will lend the store to them — run the store for a day and receive all the money from the day's sales.

Carmen and Cornel are originally from Romania. They founded Symposia in 2001. Friends and neighbors donate the treasure of books they sell. Hard covers cost $5, oversized paperbacks are $4 and paperbacks are $1 to $2.

"We accept any kind of books," Cornel said, "except encyclopedias."

1. Who are Cornel and Carmen?
   a. They are friends.
   b. They are partners.
   c. They are a couple.
   d. They are managers of the bookstore.

2. What does Symposia mean to the speaker?
   a. It is a secondhand bookstore where he can buy cheap books.
   b. It is a small theater where he can enjoy all kinds of shows.
   c. It is a community meeting place where he can meet people from all ethnic backgrounds.
   d. It is a second home to him.

3. Why do people like to go to Symposia on Wednesday nights?
   a. Because they can discuss politics and sexuality freely.
   b. Because they can discuss whatever they like.

c. Because they can make friends with all kinds of people.

d. Because they can learn a lot about other cultures.

4. Which of the following can be learned from the passage?

a. The speaker likes the atmosphere at Symposia very much, so he often goes there.

b. Carmen and Cornel are members of a charitable organization.

c. Symposia is a bookstore in name only and a community center in reality.

d. Symposia offers various programs which cater to the tastes of different people.

# Unit 7

## Non-ethical Experiments

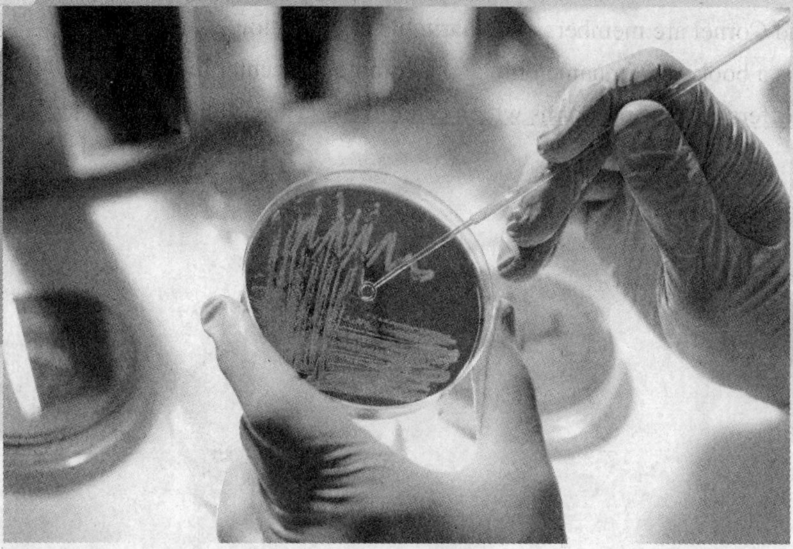

## Part A Listening Activities

### A Passage

## Never Again

Twelve people in the United States were injected with radioactive material in the 1940s — eleven with plutonium, one with uranium — to see how the body would react to an atomic bombing. At the time, scientists claimed that the people were terminally ill anyway and would not survive ten years. But a number lived longer, and one of them, Mary Connell, is still alive today. The plutonium is said to have caused thinning of the bones and other illnesses. Nine of the victims received the injections at Strong Memorial Hospital in Rochester as part of a research project conducted by the

University of Rochester and the U.S. government. The three others were injected in Illinois, California and Tennessee. Most of the victims were exposed to small amounts of radiation during experiments that were kept hidden from them.

The scientists performing the experiments had a code word for plutonium in medical records, so people couldn't figure out that these patients were injected with it. But when the tests were finally exposed in the newspapers there was a public protest, and eventually in 1996 President Bill Clinton issued a formal apology.

Yesterday the U.S. Energy Secretary formally announced a $4.8 million settlement of the issue. She said $400,000 apiece would go to families of the 11 victims now dead, and to the remaining survivor, Mary Connell — 8,000 dollars for each year she survived after being injected with radioactive uranium in medical experiments. The payments are an attempt to make up for some of the worst abuses among hundreds of similar experiments involving radiation conducted by U.S. scientists and physicians during the early days of the atomic era.

"Never again," the Energy Secretary said in announcing the settlement. "Never again should tests be performed on human beings." Doctors are unsure whether any of the 11 deaths were directly related to the experiments.

While family members and their lawyers welcomed the settlement, many, including the survivor, remain bitter about what happened. Mary Connell was given the poisonous injections while receiving treatment in the hospital for a dietary problem. She is now 73 and lives near Buffalo in the state of New York. Although pleased by the settlement she still feels as outraged about these experiments as anyone who heard about them. Luther Schultz, whose mother was injected with plutonium in November, 1945, in the same Rochester hospital, expressed strong anger over the whole shameful business. "If people had been told and knew what they were doing, it would be a different thing," he said. "But this was just picking people out and shooting poison into them."

## New Words and Expressions

radioactive /ˌreɪdɪəʊ'æktɪv/ *adj.* 放射性的 of, exhibiting, or caused by radioactivity

plutonium /pluː'təʊnɪəm/ *n.* 钚(放射性元素) a metallic radioactive element, occurring in uranium ores

uranium /jʊ'reɪnɪəm/ *n.* 铀(放射性元素) a heavy metallic radioactive element

terminally /'tɜːmɪnəlɪ/ *adv.* 晚期地，不治地 (of a disease) in the state of approaching death, unable to be cured

| | | | | |
|---|---|---|---|---|
| radiation | /ˌreɪdɪˈeɪʃən/ | *n.* | 辐射 | the process in which energy is sent out in particles or waves |
| settlement | /ˈsetlmənt/ | *n.* | (问题的)解决 | a final solution of a matter |
| apiece | /əˈpiːs/ | *adv.* | 按每个计算 | for each one |
| abuse | /əˈbjuːz/ | *v.* | 滥用 | to misuse, to use wrongly or improperly |
| dietary | /ˈdaɪətərɪ/ | *adj.* | 饮食的 | of diet |
| outraged | /ˈaʊtreɪdʒd/ | *adj.* | 激怒的 | very angry at something unjust or wrong |
| a code word | | | 代号 | a word used to keep something secret |
| make up for | | | 补偿 | to compensate, make amends |
| Mary Connell | /ˈkɒnel/ | | (女子名) | a woman's full name |
| Luther Schultz | /ˈluːθə ˈʃʊlts/ | | (男子名) | a man's full name |

## Language and Culture Notes

1. ***Background Information*** This text is adapted from an article in the *Washington Post*, in December 1996. It is believed that during the early days of the atomic age U.S. scientists conducted radiation experiments on prisoners, terminally ill patients, mentally retarded and the poor, often without their consent and without giving them due compensation. These tests were funded by the U.S. Department of Defense or the Atomic Energy Commission. According to an article in *Science News* (Oct. 29, 1994), the Advisory Committee on Human Radiation Experiments reports 400 such experiments performed between 1944 and 1974. For a long time the U.S. government remained silent and secretive about these tests. It was only in 1996 that the 12 victims or their families mentioned in the text were given their long-awaited compensation and President Clinton issued a formal apology to them.
2. ***plutonium*** A highly toxic element found in uranium ores and has an atomic number greater than that of uranium. The injection of plutonium is believed to cause the painful thinning of the bones and other diseases. Later, when the bodies of the victims injected with plutonium were examined, doctors found that their bones looked like "Swiss cheese", a hard white or pale yellow cheese with holes.

## Exercise 1

**Listen to the passage and choose the right answer for each of the following questions.**

1. What is the passage mainly about?
   a. The U.S. government and some scientists conducted secret experiments on terminally ill patients, using radioactive elements.
   b. The U.S. government committed a shameful crime, experimenting on human beings, using radioactive elements.
   c. The U.S. government promised to pay millions of dollars for experimenting on human beings, using radioactive elements.
   d. The U.S. government apologized to families of victims of secret experiments involving radioactive elements.

2. Who is Mary Connell?
   a. A woman who was injected with plutonium in the 1940s and died.
   b. A woman who was injected with uranium in the 1940s but survived.
   c. A woman who was injected with plutonium in the 1940s but survived.
   d. A woman who was injected with uranium in the 1940s and died.

3. What was the main purpose of conducting these experiments according to the passage?
   a. To find out the damaging effect of radiation on the human body.
   b. To find out the medical value of radiation.
   c. To find out how victims of radiation exposure could be cured.
   d. To find out how the human body would react to atomic bombs.

4. Which of the following did the scientists do during the experiments according to the passage?
   a. They exposed all the victims to small amounts of plutonium.
   b. They used a code name for plutonium in their medical records to avoid being detected.
   c. They did a careful study of the symptoms of the patients who were exposed to radiation.
   d. They predicted that none of the patients would survive the experiments.

5. Which of the following could be concluded from the passage?
   a. Exposure to uranium is probably not as deadly as exposure to plutonium.
   b. The scientists who conducted the experiments were no better than murderers.
   c. Exposure to uranium will do no harm to the human body.
   d. The experiments helped scientists learn a great deal about how to cope with a possible atomic war.

## Exercise 2

**Listen to the passage again and write down answers to the following questions.**

1. How many patients were injected with radioactive material in the secret experiments? How many of them are still alive today?
   *Twelve patients were injected with radioactive material and only one of them is still alive today.*
2. Where were the experiments conducted?
   *Nine of the experiments were conducted at Strong Memorial Hospital in Rochester and the other three were performed respectively in Illinois, California and Tennessee.*
3. How much money did the U.S. government promise to pay to correct the wrong it once committed? How would the money be divided among the victims or their families?
   *The U.S. government promised to pay $4.8 million, which would be shared among the eleven families of the victims and the only survivor, with each receiving $400,000.*
4. How long did Mary Connell have to wait before she was compensated for the wrong done to her?
   *Fifty years.*
5. Aside from the money, what did the U.S. government do to attempt to make up for the wrong it once committed?
   *The President of the country issued a formal apology to the victims and their families.*

# Part B Speaking Activities

### Pair Work

## Exercise 1

**Reconstruct the story of Mary Connell in your own words. Then retell it in class.**

***Guiding questions:***

1. How old was Mary Connell when she was diagnosed with a dietary problem?
2. Which hospital was she admitted to for treatment?
3. What happened to her when she was there?

4. What did the scientists claim when they selected Mary Connell and some other patients for the experiments?
5. Did the scientists' claim prove true in Mary Connell's case?
6. How many years later did the whole thing come to light?
7. How old was Mary Connell then?
8. What did she receive from President Clinton and how was she compensated for the wrong done to her?
9. Was she pleased with the settlement? How did she feel about the experiments?

***Suggested answer:***

Mary Connell was in her early twenties when she suffered from a dietary problem. She was admitted into Strong Memorial Hospital in Rochester for treatment. There, without her knowledge, she was injected with uranium in the 1940s as part of a research program conducted by the U.S. government and the University of Rochester to find out how an atomic bombing would affect the human body. The scientists who conducted the experiments claimed that she, as well as her fellow victims, could not be cured and she had only about ten years to live. However, Mary Connell survived. It was not until five decades later that the whole thing came to light. In 1996, at the age of 73, Mary Connell received a formal apology from President Clinton and $400,000 in repayment — $8,000 for each year she survived the inhuman experiment on her body. Although pleased with the settlement, she remains bitter over what was done to her and her fellow patients.

## Exercise 2

**Read the information in the chart and then discuss the questions that follow.**

| Some Important Events in the History of Human Experimentation | |
|---|---|
| **Date** | **Event** |
| **1796** | English physician Edward Jenner injects healthy eight-year-old James Phipps with cowpox（牛痘）and then a few weeks later with smallpox（天花）, proving his theory that cowpox provides protection against smallpox. His discovery is instrumental in ridding the world of the deadly disease of smallpox. |
| **1845 – 1849** | American gynecologist（妇科学家）J. Marion Sims conducts experimental operations on enslaved African women without anesthesia. |
| **1865** | French physiologist（生理学家）, Claude Bernard, publishes *An Introduction to the Study of Experimental Medicine*, in which he wrote: "Never perform an experiment which might be harmful to the patient even though highly advantageous to science or the health of others." |

(续表)

| | |
|---|---|
| 1906 | Dr. Richard Strong, a professor of tropical medicine at Harvard, experiments with cholera(霍乱) on prisoners in the Philippines, killing thirteen. |
| 1931 | Germany issues "Regulation on New Therapy and Experimentation", requiring all human experiments to be preceded by animal experiments. |
| 1931 | Germany issues guidelines on human experimentation, distinguishing between therapeutic research, intended to benefit the patient, and non-therapeutic research, intended to advance knowledge. |
| During World War II | Nazi doctors conducted horrifying experiments on inmates in concentration camps. Japanese invaders (Unit 731) conducted notorious experiments on Chinese people in the Northeast. |
| 1940 | In a program to develop new drugs to fight malaria(疟疾) during World War II, doctors in the Chicago area infected 400 prisoners with the disease. The prisoners were told that they were helping with the war effort, and not informed about the nature of the experiment. |
| 1947 | The Nuremberg Code(纽伦堡公约) sets forth ten principles to guide medical research involving human subjects. These principles include informed consent, freedom from coercion, consideration of risk and benefit, appropriate research design, and qualified investigator.<br>The Code begins with the sentence: "The voluntary consent of the human subject is absolutely essential." |
| 1964 | The World Medical Association(世界医学大会) adopts the Helsinki Declaration(赫尔辛基宣言), declaring that "the interests of science and society should never take precedence over the well being of the subject." |
| 1967 | In his book *Human Guinea Pigs: Experimentation on Man*, British physician M. H. Pappworth writes: "No physician is justified in placing science or the public welfare first and his obligation to the individual, who is his patient or subject, second. No doctor … has the right to choose martyrs for science or for the general good." |

1. In the text, the speaker describes the experiments performed on the patients as "shameful". What was ethically wrong with these experiments? (The experiments were performed on the patients without their knowledge and consent. / The experiments were not related to the diseases from which the patients were suffering and would do harm to their health. / The selection of the subjects was based on the absurd assumption that terminally ill patients would die anyway, with or without the experiments.)
2. What principles do you think doctors and scientists should follow when conducting research involving human subjects?

3. Is it right to intentionally expose some members of society to harm for the benefits of society as a whole? If yes, under what circumstances?
4. The American chemist, Edwin E. Slosson once said, "A human life is nothing compared with a new fact in science … the aim of science is the advancement of human knowledge at any sacrifice of human life." Comment.

# Part C Listen and Relax

## A Song

**Listen to the song *When a Child Is Born* and sing after the recording.**

### *When a Child Is Born*

*A ray of hope flickers in the sky*
*A tiny star lights up way up high*
*All across the land dawns a brand new morn*
*This comes to pass*
*When a child is born.*

*A silent wish sails the seven seas*
*The winds of change whisper in the trees*
*And the walls of doubt crumble, tossed and torn*
*This comes to pass*
*When a child is born.*

*A rosy hue settles all around*
*You've got the feel you're on solid ground*
*For a spell or two no one seems forlorn*
*This comes to pass*
*When a child is born.*

*(Recitation)*
*And all of this happens because the world is waiting*
*Waiting for one child*
*Black? White? Yellow? No one knows*
*But a child that will grow up*
*And turn tears to laughter*
*Hate to love, war to peace*
*And everyone to everyone's neighbor*
*And misery and suffering*
*Will be words to be forgotten forever.*

*It's all a dream and illusion now*
*It must come true sometime soon, somehow*
*All across the land dawns a brand new morn*
*This comes to pass*
*When a child is born.*

**Notes**

1. *When a Child Is Born* is the theme song in the American film *Wolf Love*, sung by the popular black singer Johnny Mathis (1935– ). The song sings of peoples longing for peace, love and laughter.
2. ***crumble, tossed and torn***: collapse

# Part D Further Listening

**Passage 1**

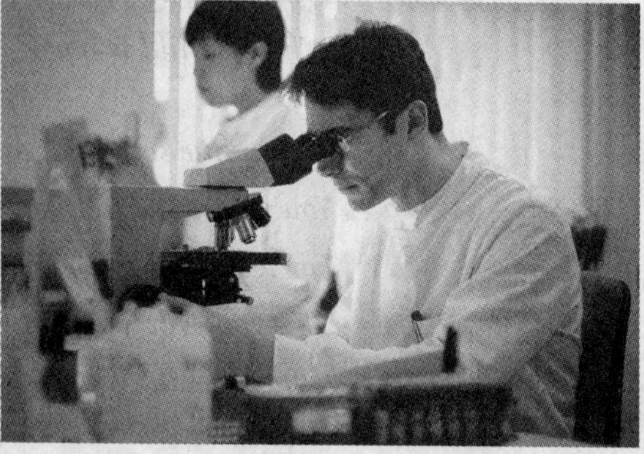

## Gregory Aller

### Exercise

**Listen to the passage carefully. Choose the right answer to each question you hear.**

Gregory was the son of Robert and Gloria Aller of Los Angeles. He suffered from a very serious mental disorder. In 1989, Gregory enrolled in a research study conducted by the University of California. Gregory had been doing well at college, earning a 3.8 grade point average and working 15 hours a week. But the study required him to stop taking the medicine for his illness. Without the medicine, he became confused and violent and lost his ability to concentrate. Years later, Robert Aller said, Gregory still has not fully recovered.

Only after a federal investigation was started did the Allers learn that more than 90 percent of those who enrolled in that experiment had also suffered from a return of their illness. They believe that if Gregory had been told about the risk, he would not have joined the study. One participant, Tony LaMadrid, did not survive the experiment. During a part of the study that did not include regular doctor visits, he jumped to his death from the roof of UCLA's engineering building.

"They claim that care in a research setting is better than the care you'd get in the community," Robert Aller said in an interview. "But LaMadrid was just seen as a source of data."

A report by the Federal Office for Protection from Research Risks criticized the study for failing to warn participants that the research was likely to cause a return of the disease. Now the Aller and LaMadrid families are suing the university.

1. What do you know about Gregory?
   a. He enrolled in the University of California in the late 1980s.
   b. He started college study in 1989.
   c. He has a serious mental illness.
   d. He became violent and lost his memory while studying in the university.

2. What was Gregory required to do during the experiment?
   a. To stop his academic study at college.
   b. To stop taking his medicine during the study.
   c. To visit his doctor daily.
   d. To take a different kind of medicine for his illness.

3. What happened to Gregory in the end?
   a. He was fully recovered.
   b. He didn't have a complete recovery.
   c. He didn't survive the experiment.
   d. He suffered from a return of his illness.

4. What are Gregory's parents doing now?
   a. They're joining the LaMadrid family to protest against the university.

b. They're suing the university.

c. They're trying to find a good lawyer to take up their case.

d. They're contacting the federal government about how the study has harmed their son's health.

**Passage 2**

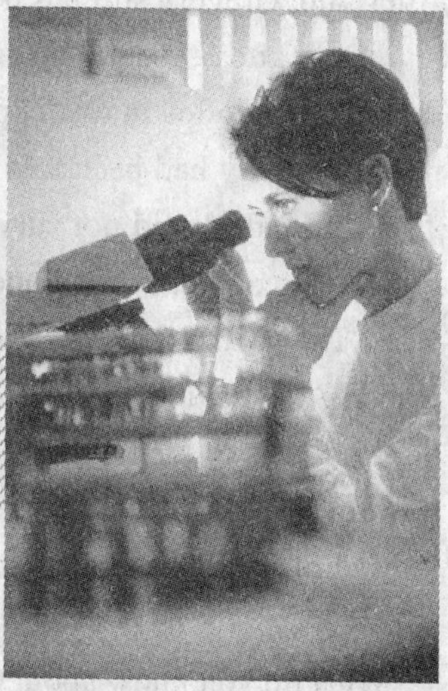

## Tuskegee Tests

### Exercise

**Listen to the passage and complete the answers to the following questions.**

In 1932, the United States Public Health Service began the Tuskegee Syphilis Study. Its aim was to observe how the disease develops when left untreated. The subjects of the investigation were 399 poor black farmers from Macon County, Alabama, with the disease, and 201 men without the disease who served as controls. The 399 men with syphilis did not realize they had the disease, as it was in its early stages. Instead of telling them they had the disease, the doctors conducting the Study lied to the men, telling them that they were being treated for "bad blood." However, they deliberately did not give the men any treatment at all. They also went to extreme lengths to make certain that the men would not receive medical treatment from any other doctors. In exchange for taking part in the Study, the men received free meals, free medical examinations, and burial insurance. The study lasted 40 years, from 1932 to 1972.

The Study casts its long shadow on today's relationship between African Americans and the medical community. Several recent articles have argued that the Study has led many African Americans to distrust medical and public health authorities. The authors point to the Study as an important factor in the low participation of African Americans in clinical trials and organ donation efforts. The distrust caused by the Study may also explain the reluctance of many black people in seeking routine preventive care.

On May 16, 1997, President Bill Clinton formally apologized to Tuskegee Study participants. Five of the eight remaining survivors of the Study took part in the White House ceremony. President Clinton said at the ceremony, "What was done cannot be undone, but we can end the silence ... We can stop turning our heads away. We can look at you in the eye, and finally say, on behalf of the American people, what the United States government did was shameful and I am sorry."

1. When did the United States Public Health Service begin the Tuskegee Syphilis Tests? And for how long?
   In *1932*. For *40 years*.
2. For what purpose did the Health Service begin the tests?
   To observe how *the disease develops when left untreated*.
3. Who joined the tests? And how many?
   *399 poor black farmers* with the disease and *201 men* without the disease who served as controls.
4. What did the doctors do to deceive the men with the disease?
   The doctors told the men with the disease that they were being treated for *"bad blood"*. And they deliberately *did not give the men any treatment at all*.
5. What's the consequence of the Study?
   It casts its long shadow on *today's relationship between African Americans and the medical community*.
6. What did President Clinton do on May 16, 1997?
   He made *a formal apology* to the Tuskegee study participants.

# Part E Home Listening

## A Compound Dictation

### Exercise

**Listen to the passage three times and supply the missing information.**

Animal testing refers to the use of animals in experiments. It is estimated that 50 to 100 million animals 1) *worldwide* — from fruit flies and mice to monkeys and apes — are used every year and either killed during the experiments or put to death afterwards. The research is carried out inside universities, medical schools, drug companies, farms, defense-research 2) *establishments*, and commercial 3) *facilities* that provide animal-testing services to industry. The great majority of laboratory animals are 4) *bred* for research purposes, while a small number are unwanted pets or animals caught in the 5) *wild*.

The earliest references to animal testing are found in the writings of the Greeks in the fourth century BC. Aristotle was one of the first to perform experiments on living animals.

The topic is controversial, however. The Foundation for Biomedical Research supports animal research. It claims that animal research has played an important role in almost every major medical 6) *advance* of the last century. Many major developments that led to Nobel Prizes involved animal research, including the development of penicillin (mice), 7) *organ* transplant (dogs), and work on polio that led to a vaccine (mice, monkeys).

Opponents argue that animal testing is unnecessary, poor scientific practice, and poorly regulated. 8) *They say the costs outweigh the benefits, and that animals have a natural right not to be used for experimentation*.

Animals have played a role in numerous well-known experiments. In the 1880s, Louis Pasteur demonstrated the germ theory of medicine by giving anthrax to sheep. 9) *In the 1890s, Ivan Pavlov famously used dogs to describe how behavior can be shaped by conditioning*. Insulin was first discovered from work on dogs in 1922, and completely changed the treatment of diabetes.10) *On November 3, 1957, a Russian dog, Laika, became the first of many animals to circle the earth*. In 1996 Dolly the sheep was born, the first mammal to be cloned from an adult cell.

## A Passage

# Non-ethical Use of Animals in Experiments

## Exercise

**Listen to the passage and fill in the table with the missing information.**

At Open University in Britain, thousands of animals are killed every year in two different areas, education and research.

Experiments are taught to students, using animals and non-ethically obtained animal tissue; that is, tissue from animals bred purposefully to be killed for students to experiment on. This is ethically wrong.

These experiments have been done for years. No new ground is broken and there are no benefits to the animals; while the same or better educational results can be obtained using video and computer simulations, self-experimentation, plants and microorganisms.

One film of one dissection or experiment can be used by thousands of students, thousands of times, and the fact that students like hands-on animal experimentation cannot justify this abuse of animals. It must stop.

If they wish to continue to use animal tissue, it must be from sources that are ethical. For example, from animals killed on roads or from donated tissue, not from animals bred just to be killed for the purpose of teaching old tricks to new students.

In medical research chickens, mice and rats are often used. These animals are used in research into human conditions. It is a practice that has been, over and over, proved to be misguided. Researchers will toil for years and years and years to find out what goes on in chickens, mice and rats. What they actually discover is what goes on in chickens, mice and rats, not in humans.

To find out what goes on in humans you must investigate humans, not animals. You can use the many humane alternatives that include computer simulation, humans after death, clinical studies, and in vitro work.

As Richard Klausner, a director at the U.S. National Cancer Institute said, "The history of curing cancer has been a history of curing cancer in the mouse. We have cured cancer in the mouse for decades — and it simply didn't work in humans."

| **Two Areas Where Animals Are Used for Experiments at OU** | |
| --- | --- |
| education | 1) *research* |
| animals and animal 2) *tissue* obtained from animals that are 3) *bred to be killed* for students to 4) *experiment on* | the practice of using 5) *chickens, rats and mice* are used in research into 6) *human conditions* |
| The practice is ethically 7) *wrong*. | The practice is 8) *misguided*. |
| can use 9) *video*, computer simulation, self-experimentation, 10) *plants and microorganisms* | can use 11) *humane alternatives* such as computer simulation, humans after death, clinical studies, and in vitro work |

# Unit 8

# Social Problems

## Part A Listening Activities

### A Radio News Story

## The Missing Student

The massive search for a missing Sannich woman today failed to turn up any trace of the 20-year-old University of Victoria student. Marguerite Tellesford disappeared last Sunday shortly after she started out for an early morning run. Police believe she was the victim of foul play. Her ear muffs and a pool of blood were found about a kilometer from her home. Barry Bell has more on the story.

Hundreds of people turned up after police called for volunteers to comb the wooded parkland of Mount Douglas, north of Victoria, for clues in the suspected murder of Marguerite Tellesford.

But four hours of painstaking probing left the searchers empty-handed. Sannich Emergency Program coordinator Lance Olmstead says the effort by the volunteers was remarkable. "Absolutely outstanding. We ended up in the end with almost three hundred people in this search. In this area 90% of the ground has been covered at least once." But Mr Olmstead says searchers found no clues or evidence in what the Sannich police are treating as a murder. The mysterious and violent disappearance of a popular student has aroused the concern of the community as expressed by those who turned up to search. Here's Victoria writer Eric Wilson: "I feel like everyone else, just wanting to help, I guess it's the first time I've lived somewhere where something like this has happened. I think everyone is very upset by it." Lauren Mallet went to junior high school and university with the missing woman. "Marguerite and I are very close friends and I just wanted to come out because I know that if I didn't ... this is just going to make me feel better." Other volunteers were Velma and Wilbur Partmiller. "My husband is 82 and I'm 77. We walk this area all the time, that's why we were so interested and so worried about her." Although the intensive search of the area where Marguerite Tellesford was last seen has officially ended, the police investigation continues, and almost ten thousand dollars in rewards have been posted for information that would lead to an arrest. The police investigation into the Marguerite Tellesford case is continuing. However, the ground search for the woman has been called off.

The twenty-year-old University of Victoria student disappeared Sunday while jogging in a heavily wooded park area in Sannich. Susan MacNamey has more on the story. "Every available person in the Sannich police department is working on this tragic case, but investigators are still baffled about the mysterious disappearance of Marguerite Tellesford. Yesterday more than four hundred volunteers turned up to take part in a massive ground search for the woman. Some of them were friends, neighbors, fellow students; others had never met Marguerite, they just wanted to help out."

And while the search failed to turn up any new evidence, Inspector Jim Arnold says the public response has been overwhelming. "We're getting all kinds of suggestions and tips from the public and, and, uh, uh, the number of volunteers that showed up is just, ... you know, is evident of the support we are getting from the community and the type of information that's coming forward." But so far none of those tips have led to any solid clues. What the police have found are the woman's ear muffs and a pool of human blood on the jogging trail. But Inspector Arnold says they haven't been able to match the blood type with that of the woman. "We have Canada Customs, and Immigration, attempting to determine from Port-of-Spain, Trinidad, where the young lady was born, her blood type, but there's no records of her pre-immigration medical and her doctor's charts and her dental charts locally and the family can't tell us what her blood type is." The reward money in this case has now climbed to over ten thousand dollars.

## *New Words and Expressions*

| | | | |
|---|---|---|---|
| massive | /ˈmæsɪv/ | *adj.* | 大规模的 large-scale |
| comb | /kəʊm/ | *v.* | 彻底搜查 to search a place very carefully |
| clue | /kluː/ | *n.* | 线索 information that helps one to find the answer to a problem or mystery |
| painstaking | /ˈpeɪnzˌteɪkɪŋ/ | *adj.* | 煞费苦心的 (of work) characterized by taking pains or trouble |
| probe | /prəʊb/ | *v.* | 调查 to examine thoroughly |
| coordinator | /kəʊˈɔːdɪneɪtə(r)/ | *n.* | 协调人 someone whose task is to see that work goes harmoniously |
| baffle | /bæfl/ | *v.* | 使困惑 to confuse, bewilder |
| overwhelming | /ˌəʊvəˈhwelmɪŋ/ | *adj.* | 极大的 very great |
| tip | /tɪp/ | *n.* | 指点，消息 a useful piece of information or advice, esp. something secret or not generally known |
| trail | /treɪl/ | *n.* | （荒野、山林中的）小径,（人或动物踩出的）小道 a path or track made across a wild region, over rough country by the passage of people or animals |
| turn up | | | （使被）找到，发现 to uncover, find |
| foul play | /faʊl/ | | 暴行（尤指谋杀） a violent criminal act, esp. murder |
| ear muffs | /mʌf/ | | 耳套 a pair of coverings for the ears |
| blood type | | | 血型 any of several types of blood a person can have |
| Marguerite Tellesford | /ˌmɑːgəˈriːt ˈtelsfɔːd/ | | （女子名） a woman's full name |
| Barry Bell | /ˈbærɪ bel/ | | （男子名） a man's full name |
| Lance Olmstead | /lɑːns ˈəʊmsted/ | | （男子名） a man's full name |
| Eric Wilson | /ˈerɪkˈwɪlsən/ | | （男子名） a man's full name |
| Lauren Mallet | /ˈlɒrenˈmælɪt/ | | （女子名） a woman's full name |
| Velma | /ˈvelmə/ | | （女子名） name (f.) |
| Wilbur Partmiller | /ˈwɪlbə(r) ˈpɑːtmɪlə/ | | （男子名） a man's full name |

| | | |
|---|---|---|
| Susan MacNamey | / ˈsuːzən məkˈnæmɪ/ | （女子名） a woman's full name |
| Jim Arnold | /dʒɪmˈɑːnəld/ | （男子名） a man's full name |
| Sannich | / ˈsænɪtʃ/ | （加拿大地名） name of a place in Victoria, Canada |
| Victoria | /vɪkˈtɔːrɪə/ | （加拿大地名） name of the capital city of British Columbia, Canada |
| Trinidad | / ˈtrɪnɪdæd/ | 特立尼达岛 name of the southernmost island in the Caribbean |

## Language and Culture Notes

1. ***Background Information*** In Western countries, crime is part of the social reality one has to live with. The crime rate is high, especially among young people. Violent crimes such as robbery, kidnapping, mugging, assault and murder often form big stories in the news. This listening text gives an account of a case of suspected murder in Victoria, Canada.
2. ***foul play*** A criminal act, especially involving murder.

## Exercise 1

**Listen to the radio news carefully. Then complete the ten sentences below according to the information you get from the recording.**

1. The massive search for a missing Sannich woman today *failed to turn up any trace* of the 20-year-old student.
2. *Her ear muffs and a pool of blood* were found about a kilometer from her home.
3. Sannich Emergency Program coordinator says *the effort by the volunteers* was remarkable.
4. *The mysterious and violent disappearance* of a popular student has aroused the concern of the community.
5. I think everyone is very *upset* by it.
6. Almost *ten thousand dollars in rewards* have been posted for information.
7. The ground search for the woman has been *called off*.
8. The 20-year-old student disappeared while *jogging in a heavily wooded park area*.
9. Some of the searchers were the woman's *friends, neighbors and fellow students*.
10. Inspector Arnold says they haven't been able to *match the blood type* with that of the missing student.

## Exercise 2

**Listen to the radio news again. Then choose the right answer to each question you hear.**

1. What probably happened to the University of Victoria student according to the police?
   a. She was kidnapped.
   b. She was murdered.
   c. She was mugged.
   d. She was assaulted.

2. What was the student doing that morning?
   a. She was walking in a quiet park.
   b. She was jogging in a street.
   c. She was working outside her home.
   d. She was jogging in an area where there were trees all round.

3. What does "massive search" mean?
   a. Search on a large scale.
   b. Search made by many volunteers.
   c. Search made by a lot of policemen.
   d. All of the above.

4. How many volunteers joined in the search for the missing woman according to Susan MacNamey?
   a. About 90.
   b. More than 100.
   c. About 300.
   d. More than 400.

5. Which of the following statements can be inferred from the news?
   a. The search was not thorough enough.
   b. The local people were very helpful.
   c. The woman was murdered near her home.
   d. The police were not competent.

# Part B Speaking Activities

## 1. Pair Work

*Reconstruct the news story of the missing student in a chronological order. Then retell it in class.*

***Guiding questions:***

1) Who was the missing student?
2) Where was she from?
3) Where was she studying?
4) What was she doing that Sunday morning?
5) What did the police find near her home?
6) What might have happened to her according to the police?
7) What did the police do to solve the mystery?
8) Who turned up to help the police with the investigation?
9) Were there any results?
10) Were the police able to identify the blood? Why or why not?
11) What was the amount of reward money in this case?

## 2. Communicative Function: Talking About Crime and Punishment

Crime is a serious social problem. Murder, robbery, burglary, theft and various other crimes threaten people's lives and property and undermine the stability of society. To combat crimes, governments put in place criminal justice system to ensure that those who choose to commit crimes are held accountable and brought to justice. Ordinary citizens, however, also need to take necessary security measures to protect themselves from crime and to assist law enforcement agencies in fighting crime when called upon.

Have you ever been a victim of crime? What are the worst forms of crime in the community where you live? What do you think the police and ordinary people can do to deal with such crimes?

What do you think are their causes? In the box below, you'll find some sentences and structures that you may find useful when talking about crime and punishment.

## TALKING ABOUT CRIME AND PUNISHMENT

Crimes can be divided into three major categories: offenses against property such as robbery, burglary, and larceny (盗窃罪), offenses against the person such as murder, rape and assault, and offenses against public safety and morals such as drunk driving, gambling and drug trafficking.

Punishments for crime may include death, imprisonment, fines, removal from public office, and disqualification from holding an office.

A person commits a crime of burglary by breaking into somebody else's home and making away with money or other valuables.

A pickpocket pretends to bump into you by accident and, without your knowing it, has lifted your wallet from your backpack.

People may get mugged when returning home from work late at night.

We must learn to protect ourselves against crime.

Some burglaries occur when people leave doors unlocked so the burglar simply walks in and steals things.

We can reduce the risk of burglary by installing a burglar alarm / by fitting burglar bars to the windows / by asking a neighbor to keep an eye on our home when we go away on holiday.

Do not let a stranger in without checking his identity / when you are alone in the house.

When we go shopping in a crowded place, we should be especially alert / guard against pickpockets / keep an eye on our wallet or purse / keep our money and valuables out of sight / should never leave our bag unattended.

The best defense against pickpockets is to make it hard for them to get to your valuables.

Avoid walking alone at night / narrow alleys or poorly-lit streets.

If you are followed by a vehicle, you should never try to outrun it. Instead, turn around and walk quickly in the opposite direction.

If we happen to spot someone committing a crime, we should alert the police / dial 110 to call the police.

We need more police presence / patrolling in the neighborhood.

We need to take tough measures to reduce / control / crack down on crime.

An effective way to deter crime is to impose harsh penalties on lawbreakers /

offenders / those who commit crimes / those who violate the law.

Poverty, unemployment, lack of education, broken homes, growing material needs and the huge gap between the rich and the poor are among the problems that breed crime.

Only by addressing the underlying root causes of crime can we succeed in controlling crime.

## A Model

**Lisa** Jane, have you heard that there have been a series of overnight burglaries in the neighborhood of our school recently?

**Jane** Really?

**Lisa** They say that in each case, burglars broke into a home while the victims were sleeping and got away with wallets, cell phones and laptops.

**Jane** Were these burglaries linked?

**Lisa** Probably. A reward of $10,000 has been posted by the police for information. The police also urge residents of the area to make sure that their windows are closed and their doors locked before they go to bed.

**Jane** Well, it's common sense to lock up at night, but sometimes people are just not careful enough. There was a program on TV last week about a man who was arrested and convicted of burglary. He said he managed to get into people's home simply by trying doors from home to home to see if they were left unlocked.

**Lisa** With the rising crime rate, we really need to be more alert. At my home, we always leave a light on when we go out at night as if there were someone at home.

**Jane** That's a good way to deter burglars. Most burglars are opportunists. They are looking for easy targets. If they think it's too risky or too difficult to break into a home, they'll just move on and try another one.

**Lisa** But why do you think there are so many burglars around in the first place? I read in the newspaper that the number of burglaries is on the rise in many cities across the country.

**Jane** I think a major reason is that we have a very large migrant population. More and more people are moving to the cities in search of a better life, but jobs, especially decently paid jobs are hard to find. Then some of them might be tempted to try to get money through unlawful means such as theft and burglary.

**Lisa** Indeed, unemployment, poverty and the huge gap in income, these things are at the root of many crimes. We really have to address these issues if we want to reduce burglary and other

more violent crimes.

**Jane** Exactly.

*Now try to use what you've learned in this lesson and carry out the following tasks.*

1) Describe to your partner a crime that has happened to you or to someone you know.
2) Work in groups of three or four. Discuss what crimes happen most frequently in the community where you live. Do you have any suggestions as to how to combat these crimes? What do you think are the causes of these crimes?

# *Part C* *Listen and Relax*

## A Song

**Listen to the song *Nobody's Child* and sing after the recording.**

### *Nobody's Child*

*As I was slowly passing an orphans' home one day,*
*and stopped there for a moment just to watch the children play.*
*Alone a boy was standing and when I asked him why,*
*he turned with eyes that could not see and he began to cry.*
*"I'm nobody's child. I'm nobody's child,*
*just like a flower I'm growing wild.*
*No mommy's kisses and no daddy's smile,*
*nobody wants me, I'm nobody's child.*

*People come for children and take them for their own,*
*but they all seem to pass me and I'm here alone.*
*I know they'd like to take me, but when they see I'm blind,*
*they always take some other child and I'm left behind.*

*No mommy's arms to hold me,*
*or soothe me when I cry.*

*Sometimes it gets so lonely,*
*I wish that I could die.*
*I'd walk the streets of heaven, where all the blind can see,*
*and just like all the other kids there'll be a home for me."*

# Part D Further Listening

**A Passage**

## Divorce and Remarriage

### Exercise

**You are going to hear a passage. Listen carefully and choose the right answer to each question you hear.**

In many homes, divorce is caused by the "battle between the sexes". To understand the problem, one must remember the modern American woman is freed. During childhood and adolescence, the American girl is given freedom and education which is equal to a boy's. After completing school, she is able to get a job and support herself. She doesn't have to marry for financial security. She considers herself an independent, self-sufficient person. She wants a husband whom she can respect, but she doesn't want to be dominated by him. She wants a democratic household in which she has a voice in making decisions. When a husband and wife are able to share decision-making, their marriage is probably closer, stronger, and more satisfying. Otherwise, the couple is likely to wind up in the divorce court.

When a couple gets divorced, the court usually requires the man to pay his former wife a monthly sum of money. If the couple has children, they usually remain with the mother, and the father is expected to pay for their support.

Although divorce is quite common in the United States, 80 percent of those who get divorced

remarry. The remarriages allow thousands of people, especially children, to enjoy family life again, but at the same time many troubles have arisen. A well-known American joke tells of a wife calling to her second husband, "Quick, John! Come here and help me! Your children and my children are beating up our children!"

1. What causes most of the divorce cases in the U.S.A.?
   a. Financial trouble in the family.
   b. Women's liberation movement.
   c. Different attitudes between husband and wife towards children's education.
   d. Lack of democratic atmosphere in the household.

2. What do you know of modern American women, according to the passage?
   a. They are overbearing.
   b. They are independent and able to support themselves.
   c. They do not have much say in the household.
   d. They respect their husbands, but do not listen to them.

3. What kind of marriage can be successful?
   a. Both the man and woman are financially secure.
   b. Husband and wife share housework.
   c. Decisions are made by the man and woman together.
   d. Both the man and woman are well-educated.

4. What happens when a couple is divorced, according to the passage?
   a. The children become homeless.
   b. The man is responsible for the welfare of his children.
   c. Life becomes difficult for the woman and her children.
   d. The man, rather than the woman, remarries soon.

5. What does the well-known joke suggest?
   a. Remarriages often end up in failure.
   b. Children are unhappy in the new family.
   c. The mother cannot get along with her stepchildren.
   d. Remarriages cause new troubles in the household.

## A Compound Dictation

### Exercise

**Listen to the passage three times and supply the missing information.**

Bill, a college student says, "I have been using the Internet for about four years. Now I spend most of the day on-line. I'm trying to 1) _cut_ my hours, but I simply don't have the 2) _strength_ to. I'm like an 3) _alcoholic_ who can't control his habit." For years, people have been addicted to things like nicotine, gambling, or drinking. However, now a new 4) _high-tech_ addiction called Internet addiction is rapidly becoming the latest problem of the computer age.

College and university students, businesspeople, and 5) _homemakers_ are just some of the people who are spending hours and hours in front of their computer 6) _screens_. They are sending e-mails, playing computer games, or entering 7) _chat-rooms_ where they can communicate with strangers all over the world on their computer.

At first, these individuals went on-line for work, study, or pleasure and spent one or two hours a day on their computer. However, the hours gradually increased. They began to surf the Net for longer and longer periods of time.

Bill's 8) _compulsiveness, his inability to stop thinking about his on-line activity, turned into a serious psychological problem_. He gave up his friends, stopped playing basketball, and neglected his schoolwork. Instead he found fulfillment by communicating electronically with strangers.

Psychologists have become concerned about this growing problem. 9) _They feel that Internet addicts are avoiding the intimacy that comes from live, non-electronic communication_. Counselors worry that students will not go through the normal social developmental stages. As a result, at many colleges, 10) _counseling centers are now offering support groups, a special form of therapy that is helping these students control their on-line habit_.

# Part E Home Listening

## A Passage

### Teenage Drinking

#### Exercise

**You are going to hear a passage. Listen carefully and choose the right answer to each question you hear.**

Today American parents are finding themselves in a dilemma about how to deal with teenage drinking, a serious social problem. A recent survey has revealed that 92% of high school seniors have tried alcohol at least once and two-thirds take a drink once a month. Alcohol has resulted in a lot of teenage car crashes, as well as suicides and murders. Parents are wondering why they can't keep their children from drinking. Now many are beginning to conclude that it is not the kids but the parents who should be held responsible for their permissive attitudes.

Some parents find that stern attitudes and methods are impractical and ineffective. They try to teach their children to drink responsibly and moderately. Many parents believe that supervised drinking is a safe solution.

However, an increasing number of parents fear that this will endanger their children's safety. Therefore, hardliners are striving to form a united front to lay down common rules to be strictly enforced. And the most popular method in some communities is what they call "safe homes", where unsupervised parties with alcohol are forbidden. The hardliners think that in this way their children will learn self-control. But experts and educators fear that such attitudes might invite outright rebellion from the children. Both sides agree that teenage-drinking can be dealt with if no excessive drinking attitudes are established early and supported by school authorities.

1. Why is teenage drinking said to be a serious problem according to the passage?
   a. Because it involves a very high percentage of high school students.
   b. Because it is usually connected with drunk-driving.
   c. Because it has resulted in traffic accidents and deaths.
   d. Because it is harmful to the health of the children.

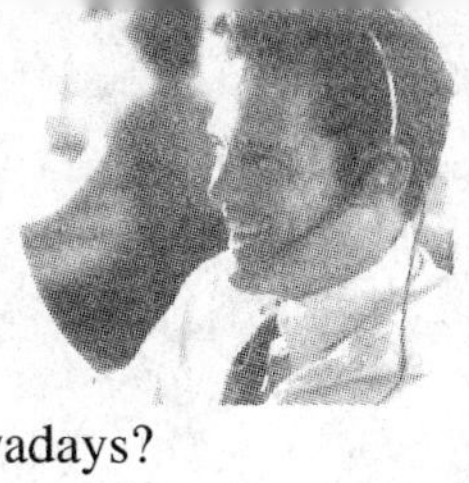

2. Who should be held responsible for teenage drinking according to many people nowadays?
   a. The young people themselves.
   b. Parents who are too permissive.
   c. School authorities.
   d. The permissive society.

3. Which of the following measures by parents is NOT mentioned?
   a. To teach their children to drink moderately.
   b. To hold stern attitudes and use severe methods.
   c. To strive to have some strict rules enforced.
   d. To give less pocket money to their children.

4. What is a "safe home"?
   a. A home where teenagers are not allowed to drink alcohol.
   b. A place where drinking of alcohol at parties is supervised.
   c. A community where drinking is supervised.
   d. A place where parties with alcohol are forbidden.

5. How can teenage drinking be dealt with, according to experts and educators?
   a. Drinking should be supervised in every community.
   b. No alcohol should be sold to teenagers.
   c. Correct attitudes towards drinking are established early and supported by authorities.
   d. Teenagers should only go to "safe homes".

## A Compound Dictation

### Exercise

**Listen to the passage three times and supply the missing information.**

Indians in the United States are faced with 1) *significant* problems. Many Indians still live on reservations. They don't even have indoor 2) *plumbing*. The water there is often so contaminated that it is not 3) *fit* for drinking. Mechanization has gradually 4) *eliminated* many of the ranching and agricultural jobs 5) *formerly* available to the Indians, and few industries have been set up on the reservations. In any case, most native Americans have had only very little schooling and remain 6) *untrained* for skilled jobs. Among some tribes, the unemployment rate 7) *exceeds* 50 percent, and about 80 percent of the people must rely on some form of government assistance.

Indians have their own languages and cultures, and each tribe wants to keep up its traditions and preserve some of its native customs. 8) *The adults want their children to be proud of being Indians, as well as to survive in the modern world*. The young people on their part, want to enter the world that they see every day on television and in the movies. Like everyone else, they are anxious to get a good education and a good job. However, 9) *they have little prospect for success and become very frustrated because they usually can only go to inferior schools and often find it impossible to adjust to present-day life*. In addition, they feel that they are discriminated against, and this makes them lose much of their confidence and pride. 10) *The most important problem that American Indians have to tackle is the restoring of their pride and self-confidence.* And this is to be first and foremost if they are to change their destiny.

# Unit 9

# Use of Technology

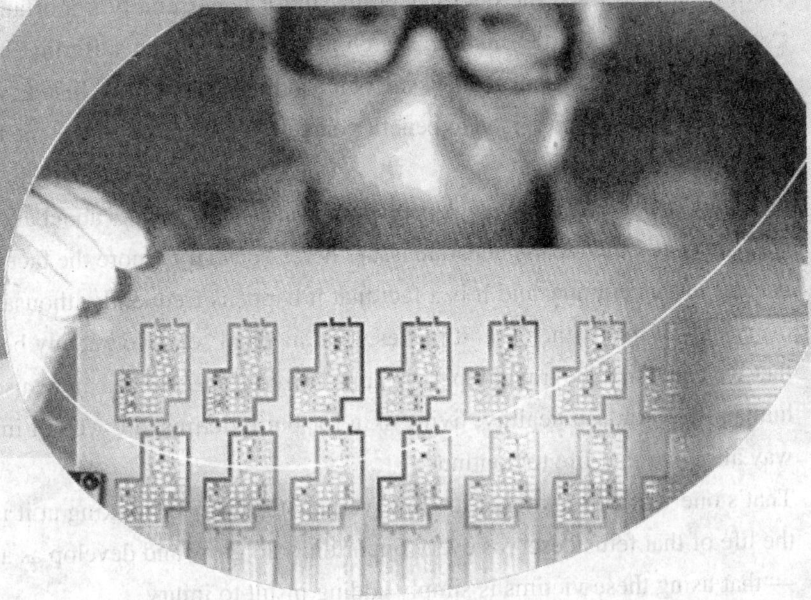

## Part A Listening Activities

### A Debate

## Seeing Both Sides

**Host** Good morning, and welcome to today's program of *Seeing Both Sides*. Today we have something very interesting for you — a very controversial topic. Is it a moral use of technology to take advantage of fetal tissue for medical experimentation? Our guests today are Dr Kim Benson, head of the organization of Physicians for Responsible Research, and Mr William Cooper. They're here to discuss the moral and medical implications of this new area of research. Dr Benson, let's begin by hearing your view.

**Dr Benson** Well, scientifically speaking, it's clear that fetal tissue is quite a gold mine. It's been proven to be extremely successful in grafting new tissue for use with burn victims. Research is being done into other potential uses as well.

**Host** Mr Cooper, how do you respond to that?

**Mr Cooper** Well, of course I see the doctor's point, and it is extremely important that we do everything possible in terms of research to alleviate human suffering; however, you can't ignore the fact that fetal tissue is a product of abortion. Just as we hope you would not kill another person to benefit yourself, it is immoral to use the life of a fetus in this way.

**Dr Benson** Yes, Mr Cooper, I suppose some people may have strong views about abortion but it's really important to clearly separate issues here. You can't ignore the fact that abortion is legal in this country and it is a fact that it happens frequently, thousands of times every day. If this is the case, it makes good medical sense to get any benefit from it that we can. Isn't the tragedy perhaps minimized if this tissue can be used to further human life? And, in healthy, living skin for burn victims, are we not in some small way allowing that life to continue?

**Mr Cooper** That's one way of looking at it. However, another way of looking at it is to say that the life of that fetus deserves every opportunity to grow and develop as an individual — that using these victims is simply adding insult to injury.

**Dr Benson** Maybe you have a point there, and I'm sure many people would agree with you, but the flip side of the issue is that our greatest moral obligation is to the living. As long as abortion is legal, as long as those fetuses are not developing into full-fledged human life, it seems we must devote our energies to concentrating on and helping in every way possible those who are alive and suffering.

**Host** You've both raised a number of very interesting points. I'm sure you've given our listeners a lot of food for thought about this complex and controversial issue. Let's take a break now and when we return we'll take some calls from our listeners.

## New Words and Expressions

| | | | |
|---|---|---|---|
| controversial | /ˌkɒntrəˈvɜːʃəl/ | *adj.* | 有争议的 causing disagreement |
| fetal | /ˈfiːtəl/ | *adj.* | 胚胎的 of fetus, which is a human being or animal developing in the mother's uterus before it is born |
| tissue | /ˈtɪʃjuː/ | *n.* | （动植物的）组织 the substance that animal and plant cells are made of |

| | | | |
|---|---|---|---|
| graft | /grɑ:ft/ | *v.* | 移植 to cut a healthy piece of skin, tissue or bone from a person's own body and use it to repair a damaged part on that person |
| alleviate | /ə'li:vɪeɪt/ | *v.* | 减轻，缓和 to make something less painful, severe or serious |
| abortion | /ə'bɔ:ʃən/ | *n.* | 人工流产 a medical operation in which a developing baby is removed from a woman's womb so that it is not born alive |
| issue | /'ɪʃju:/ | *n.* | 讨论或争议中的问题或争论点 a subject that people discuss or argue about |
| further | /'fɜ:ðə(r)/ | *v.* | 增进 to help something to succeed |
| fledged | /fledʒd/ | *adj.* | 羽翼丰满的 with feathers that are developed enough for flying |
| burn victim | | | 烧伤病人 someone who has been injured by fire |
| make good medical sense | | | 从医学角度上讲，非常合情合理 quite meaningful from medical point of view |
| in some small way | | | 小规模 on a small scale |
| the flip side | | | 反面 the opposite or less attractive side of an idea, plan or situation |
| Kim Benson | /kɪm 'bensən/ | | （男子名） a man's full name |
| Physicians for Responsible Research | | | 内科医生重大责任研究学会 name of an organization of physicians |
| William Cooper | /'ku:pə/ | | （男子名） a man's full name |

## Language and Culture Notes

1. ***Background Information*** Technology is the application of scientific knowledge for practical purposes. It has affected society and its surroundings in many ways, both positively and negatively. Modern civilization depends greatly on technology. Since 1974, technology in medicine has supplied hospitals, integrated healthcare systems, and alternate care delivery sites with the highest quality clinical engineering and medical equipment maintenance.

There are two sides to every question. The same holds true in the use of technology in medicine. Take stem cell research, for example. Using fetal tissues and their basic cells — stem cells— for medical research purposes is a fast growing and very promising branch of biology. These tissues are obtained through abortion or stillbirth. The stem cells have the ability to reproduce rapidly and to specialize into any of the body's tissue types, including the skin, liver, kidneys, or brain. This makes them highly adaptable and less likely to be rejected by a transplant recipient. Cells from fetal tissue grow much faster than cells from the tissue of adults, and they are easier to culture in the laboratory and in greater supply than adult tissue. Therefore, they have great potential in treating certain hitherto incurable and life-threatening diseases. There is, however, much debate concerning the ethic aspects of using fetal tissues in medical research. In the conversation, Dr Benson and Mr Cooper represent the two sides of the debate.

2. ***Abortion*** Abortion was legalized in the United States in 1973. The U.S. Supreme Court ruled that women, in consultation with their physicians, have a constitutionally protected right to have an abortion in the early stages of pregnancy. In 1992, the Court reaffirmed the right to abort. The data in 2006 showed that 24% of all pregnancies end in abortion. Women also have the right to terminate their pregnancy in many parts of the world, including Britain (legalized in 1967), Canada, and many other countries. Almost 2/3 of the world's women currently reside in countries where abortion may be obtained on request, for a broad range of social, economic or personal reasons. However, there are a lot of pro-life groups around the world who are very much opposed to abortion. Mr Cooper in the conversation holds the view of such groups.
3. ***If this is the case*** If the situation you describe is accurate
4. ***Maybe you have a point there*** Perhaps what you have said is reasonable

## Exercise 1

**Listen to the discussion and choose the right answer to each question you hear.**

1. What is the complex and controversial topic in today's discussion?
   a. The use of technology in medicine.
   b. <u>The use of fetal tissue for medical experimentation.</u>
   c. Whether fetal tissue is a product of abortion or not.
   d. The potential uses of fetal tissue in medicine.
2. What does Dr Benson think of abortion?
   a. It is an act of murder, and it is illegal.

b. It is used to benefit some people, but it is immoral.
c. It is legal, and it happens frequently.
d. It can help alleviate human suffering, and it is moral.

3. What is Mr Cooper's viewpoint of fetus growth?
   a. Fetus can grow and develop as an individual.
   b. Fetus can not develop into full-fledged human life.
   c. Fetus can grow to a certain extent, and then stop growing.
   d. Fetus can have some opportunities to grow, but the opportunities are very few.

4. What does Dr Benson advocate at the end of the discussion?
   a. Doctors must try to use fetal tissues on burn victims.
   b. Doctors must not kill a person to benefit another person.
   c. Doctors must devote their energies to medical experiments.
   d. Doctors must make great efforts to help those people who are still alive but suffering.

5. Which of the following can be concluded from the discussion?
   a. The use of human fetus in medical experiment will enable doctors to find a cure for cancer and other deadly diseases.
   b. The use of technology in medicine needs to be carefully examined.
   c. The use of fetus tissues with burn victims will be adopted more often.
   d. The use of technology in medical experiments must not be encouraged.

## Exercise 2

**Listen to the discussion again and complete the viewpoints expressed by Dr Benson and Mr Cooper.**

**Dr Benson**

1. Scientifically speaking, it's clear that *fetal tissue is quite a gold mine*. It's been proven to be extremely successful in grafting *new tissue for use with burn victims*.
2. You can't ignore the fact that *abortion is legal* in this country and it is a fact that it happens *frequently*, thousands of times every day. If this is the case, it *makes good medical sense to get any benefit from it* that we can.
3. The *flip* side of the issue is that *our greatest moral obligation is to the living*. As long as abortion is legal, as long as those fetuses are not developing into full-fledged human life, it seems we must

*devote our energies to concentrating and helping in every way possible those who are alive and suffering*.

**Mr Cooper**

1. You can't ignore the fact that *fetal tissue is a product of abortion*.
2. Just as we hope you would not kill another person to benefit yourself, *it is immoral to use the life of a fetus in this way*.
3. The life of that fetus *deserves every opportunity to grow and develop as an individual* — that using these victims is simply *adding insult to injury*.

# Part B Speaking Activities

## Pair Work

### Exercise 1

**Dr Benson and Mr Cooper represent the two sides of the debate over fetal tissue research. Summarize in your own words the arguments each puts forward to defend his position on the issue. You may use the following guiding questions to help you organize your answer.**

**For Dr Benson**

1. What does Dr Benson say about the scientific and medical value of fetal tissue?
2. What example does he give to illustrate his point?
3. Why does he think that the issue of fetal tissue research should be separated from the issue of abortion?
4. According to Dr Benson, in what way can fetal tissue research lessen the tragedy of abortion?
5. In Dr Benson's opinion, what is our greatest moral obligation and under what circumstances are we justified to use fetal tissue to fulfill that obligation?

**For Mr Cooper**

1. What is Mr Cooper's view on scientific research aimed at reducing human suffering?

2. Why does he oppose fetal tissue research?
3. What does he say about using fetal tissue in medical research?

*Now whose argument do you find more persuasive? Why?*

## Exercise 2

**In an argument or debate, sometimes it's a good strategy to respond to your opponent's argument by giving it the credit it deserves before you make your counterargument. Listen to the recording again and note how Dr Benson and Mr Cooper both employ this strategy in their exchange of views. You may want to refer to the following:**

Well, of course I see the doctor's point, and it is extremely important that we do everything possible in terms of research to alleviate human suffering; *however*, you can't ignore the fact that fetal tissue is a product of abortion. (Mr Cooper)

Yes, Mr Cooper, I suppose some people may have strong views about abortion *but* it's really important to clearly separate issues here. (Dr Benson)

That's one way of looking at it. *However*, another way of looking at it is ... (Mr Cooper)

Maybe you have a point there, and I'm sure many people would agree with you, *but* the flip side of the issue is ... (Dr Benson)

The above sentences are good examples of the rhetorical strategy called "concession and refutation(让步与反驳)." This strategy can strengthen your argument because it shows that you are familiar with the opposing viewpoints and that your argument is the result of a careful consideration of both sides of the issue under discussion. It also serves to build a friendly atmosphere and helps to establish your credibility as a reasonable, intelligent and respectful person who is willing to listen to opposing views.

*Now debate the following topic. Try to use the strategy of "concession and refutation" in your debate.*

Advances in genetics may make it possible for parents to "select" their children's genes and characteristics. Are you for or against the creation of genetically modified or designer babies? You may want to consider the following:

**Arguments for the creation of designer babies**

Genes that are linked to certain hereditary or other diseases can be replaced to ensure that the baby and future generations won't have these diseases.

Genetic modification may enable parents to have babies better in appearance, intelligence, character, etc.

Genetic engineering can increase the human's chances of survival as a species in the natural world.

**Arguments against the creation of designer babies**

The consequences of adding, removing, altering genes are unpredictable. Any mistake would be permanent.

Parents have no right to select the traits they desire for their child without the child's consent.

The quest to create a perfect baby can lead to a decrease of human diversity.

Those whose parents could not afford to genetically engineer them may be disadvantaged, leading to new forms of inequality.

Genetic modification turns a human being into a manufactured product.

# Part C Listen and Relax

## Riddles in Rhyme

**You're going to hear three riddles in rhyme. Supply the missing words and guess what they are.**

(1)

*It doesn't have any taste, color or smell.*
*It doesn't have any arms or legs, but it can run.*
*It isn't alive, but it's full of life.*
*You can find it everywhere around an island.*
*What is it? Water*

(2)

*We're very large though we seem small.*

*We float on <u>high</u> and never <u>fall</u>.*
*We <u>shine</u> like <u>jewels</u> in the night.*
*But in the day we are <u>hid from sight</u>.*
*Please guess what we are.* ***Stars***

(3)

*Take away my first letter,*
*Take away my second letter,*
*Take away <u>all my letters</u>.*
*And I still <u>remain the same</u>.*
*What am I?* ***A postman***

# Part D Further Listening

**Passage 1**

## How Computers Help Firefighters

### Exercise

**You are going to hear a passage. Listen carefully and choose the right answer to each question you hear.**

In Kansas City, Missouri, a computer helps firefighters. The computer contains information about every one of the 350,000 street addresses in the city. When a firefighter answers a call, the computer gives him information about the burning building. The computer can give the location of the building and its size, type and content.

In fact, the computer system has almost unlimited ways of helping firefighters with their problems. For example, it can give medical information about invalids living in a burning building. With this information the firefighters can take special care to find these sick persons and remove

them quickly and safely. The speed of a computer is amazing. Within 2 or 3 seconds after a call is received, the computer provides necessary information for the firefighters. The information is then sent to them by radio from the computer center in the city hall.

The Kansas City computer system also contains a medical record of each of the city's 900 firefighters. This kind of information is especially useful when a firefighter is injured. With this medical information doctors of a hospital can treat the injured firefighters more quickly and easily. The firefighters themselves greatly appreciate the help from the computer. They know about possible dangers ahead of them and can prepare for them. Many times the computer information helps to save lives and properties, and sometimes the lives of the firefighters themselves.

1. Which of the following is NOT included in the computer information?
   a. The location and the size of a burning building.
   b. The type and the content of a burning building.
   c. The cause of the fire.
   d. The residents' addresses.

2. How is information about a fire sent to the firefighters?
   a. By the computer installed in the fire engine.
   b. By telephone.
   c. By television.
   d. By radio.

3. How many firefighters are there in Kansas City?
   a. 9,000. b. 900.
   c. 800. d. 3,500.

4. What is the main idea of the passage?
   a. The computer is of some use in putting out fires.
   b. The computer is of great use in finding invalids.
   c. The computer is of great use in rescuing injured firefighters.
   d. The computer is a great help to firefighters.

5. What can you infer from the passage?
   a. Firefighters in Kansas City are more likely to be cured of injuries now than before.
   b. Firefighters can hardly rescue the sick trapped in a burning building without the computer.
   c. The danger for firefighters is sometimes greater than that for people in a burning building.
   d. Fires happen frequently in Kansas City.

**Passage 2**

# Dozens of Problems at Quake-hit Plant

## Exercise

**Listen to the passage carefully. Complete the following chart with the missing information you've got from the recording.**

A long list of problems — including radiation leaks, burst pipes and fires — came to light at the world's largest nuclear power plant, a day after it was hit by a powerful earthquake on July 16, 2007. The problems and a delay in reporting them increased concerns about the safety of Japan's 55 nuclear reactors, which have suffered a series of accidents and cover-ups.

The plant, which generates 8.2 million kilowatts of electricity, is the world's largest nuclear power plant. But since its start, it has been troubled with problems. In 2001, a radioactive leak was found in the turbine room of one reactor. This time the power plant suffered broken pipes, water leaks and spills of radioactive waste when the earthquake hit it on Monday.

Signs of problems, however, came first not from the officials, but in a cloud of smoke that rose up when the quake started a small fire at an electrical transformer.

It was announced only 12 hours later that the quake also caused a leak of about 315 gallons of water containing radioactive material. Officials said the water leak was well within safety standards. The water was flushed into the sea. Later Tuesday, it said 50 faults had been found. Officials insisted there was no harm to the environment, but admitted it took a day to discover about 100 drums of low-level nuclear waste that were overturned, some with the lids open. A spokesman for Tokyo Electric Power Co., which runs the plant, called the problems "minor troubles".

For residents, thousands of whom work at the plant, the worries over its safety added to already severe problems. These included heavy rains and the threat of landslides, water and power outages, and poor communications.

Japan's nuclear plants supply about 30 percent of the country's electricity, but its dependence on nuclear power is coupled with deep concern over safety. Environmentalists have criticized Japan's reliance on nuclear energy as foolish in a nation that suffers from such powerful quakes.

| Information About the Plant | |
|---|---|
| The plant | It generates 1) *8.2 million* kilowatts of electricity, and is the world's 2) *largest nuclear power* plant. |
| Its problems | a. In 2001 3) *a radioactive leak* was found in the turbine room of one reactor.<br>b. In 2007 it was hit by a powerful earthquake and the plant suffered 4) *broken pipes*, water leaks and spills of 5) *radioactive waste*. There was also a leak of 6) *315* gallons of water containing 7) *radioactive material*. |
| Officials' reactions | 8 ) *Delay in reporting the problems*;<br>They said:<br>a. the water leak was 9) *well within safety standards*;<br>b. there was no harm to 10) *the environment*.<br>A spokesman called the problems 11) *minor troubles*. |
| Reactions of residents | They are worried over the plant's 12) *safety* as well as problems of heavy rains, the threat of landslides, 13) *water and power outages and poor communications*. |

## Part E Home Listening

### A Compound Dictation

#### Exercise

**Listen to the passage three times and supply the missing information.**

Everybody knows that car is a 1) *marvelous* machine. The experts 2) *predict* that cars of the future will be made of 3) *plastic* and carbon fibers that will be much stronger than steel and much lighter in 4) *weight*. Even the engines will be made of these materials.

Cars of the future will be smaller and lighter but their designs will probably be 5) *similar* to those of the latest 6) *models* of the modern sports cars. There will probably not be any

7) *extreme* design changes for a long time.

The real frontier for cars of the future lies not in body design but with computer activation. 8) *Cars may someday actually drive themselves*. Highways would probably be wired so that cars could be programmed to travel a certain route and make the trip with or without a driver. 9) *Everyone in the car would be able to relax, even take a nap, as the car speeds along at hundreds of kilometers per hour*. The car would be radar- and computer-controlled to never touch other driverless cars, trucks or buses on the road. Changes of destination along the way could be made from a computer in the car to a central computer controlling and regulating the traffic.

10) *Most automobile designers and engineers believe that such cars are certain to be built in the future, perhaps, even as early as the early 21st century* — which would make it in your lifetime.

## A Passage

# Leave a Computer On All the Time or Shut It Off When You're Done?

### Exercise

**Listen to the passage and decide whether the statements you hear after the passage are true (T) or false (F).**

Years ago the conventional wisdom was that leaving your computer on all the time would allow it to last longer before a crash. Frequent starts and stops would cause your hard drive mechanism to wear out much faster than if the drive never spun down. An old saying was that stopping and restarting a hard drive was the same as eight hours of regular running time.

I talked to the good folks at Seagate to find out if things had changed. According to the company, starting and stopping is not a huge problem with drives any more, and they can be safely shut off and on in order to save power. According to Seagate, you can expect a drive to last for three to five years of running time before dying, though obviously many drives last longer.

What's the big factor that causes drives to die early? Heat, says Seagate. Making sure your computer stays cool through the proper use is by far the best thing you can do to keep your drive healthy. I'd imagine that shutting it down when not in use will only help. Naturally, shutting down

your computer will also conserve electricity, so unless there's a compelling reason to leave it on (as with a server), you should probably shut down at night.

So, how should you shut down properly? It's completely up to you, really. If you do a full "Shut Down" (or "Turn Off Computer") your computer will be completely off, using no power at all. On the other hand, "Hibernate" and "Standby" are lower-power states that allow you to resume quickly into the Windows desktop. Standby simply powers down hardware components like the hard drive, monitor, and peripherals, but continues to provide power to RAM, so everything you were doing stays active. Hibernate is closer to a shut down: It saves an exact image of your Windows desktop, then powers the PC down. When you awaken from hibernation, everything is back where you last had it. Personally I'm not a big fan of hibernate, because if I'm going to shut Windows down completely I like to reload everything fresh into RAM, which helps system stability. I tend to use both standby (for shorter times away from my PC) and shut down (for more than a few hours of downtime) instead.

1. Frequent starts and stops of your computer is still believed to cause the hard drive mechanism to crash. ( F )
2. According to Seagate you can obviously expect a drive to last for about five years of running time before dying. ( T )
3. It is heat that causes drives to die early. ( T )
4. The main reason why we should shut down our computers when not in use is to save electricity. ( F )
5. Hibernate and Standby can help you resume into the Windows desktop quickly. ( T )
6. The speaker favors Standby when he is not using his computer for more than a few hours. ( F )

# Unit 10

# Luck

## Part A Listening Activities

### A Conversation

#### Lucky Charms

*Four young people, Mary, Sarah, Dave and Bob, are talking about lucky charms.*

**Mary** Sarah, here are your keys back, thanks. What's that horn on your key ring for?

**Sarah** Oh, it's a souvenir from Italy, Mary. I got it last year when we were there on holiday. It's supposed to bring good luck, but it doesn't seem to be working so far! I suppose I did win a tenner on the lottery a couple of weeks ago, but that's about it.

**Dave** Gullible tourists! It's all a racket to make money! You make your own luck in this world.

**Sarah** Well, how come people have been carrying around lucky charms with them for so long

then? I mean, the Egyptians have been carrying scarabs around and wearing them as jewellary for thousands of years. I think the ancient Egyptians believed that they'd protect them from death and people who died were buried with them.

**Dave** How come you know so much, Sarah?

**Sarah** I'm interested in things like that. Oh, Mary, do you know that people in India wear peacock feathers on their clothes to keep evil away?

**Mary** That's interesting because peacock feathers are supposed to bring bad luck and you shouldn't have any in your house. The eye pattern on them is supposed to be the evil eye. I remember my brother picking one up once and bringing it home and my mum wouldn't let him keep it because it was unlucky.

**Bob** Hmm. I've never heard about that but I know that the eye thing is quite popular in Turkey. You see them all over the place there. People hang them in their houses and in their cars and they're supposed to protect you from the evil eye and bad luck.

**Sarah** I've seen them — they're really pretty, aren't they?

**Dave** It's all a load of mumbo jumbo. A friend of mine went out with a Japanese girl when we were at university and she had this little cat statue which went everywhere with her. It had one arm up in the air which was supposed to attract good luck but she dropped it one day and the arm came off. You should have seen the state she got into over it. Just a silly little thing like that. What's the point?

**Sarah** Well, everyone's allowed to have their own beliefs, aren't they? I bet, Dave, you've got a lucky pair of socks or something you wear if you've got a special date or an interview or something!

**Dave** I haven't.

**Mary** I've got a little dragon brooch that I wear sometimes. A Chinese friend of mine gave it to me years ago and told me it would protect me against unhappiness and the loss of love. I should have been wearing it the night Phil told me he didn't want to see me any more.

**Dave** There you are, you see — not a very lucky charm, is it, Mary?

**Mary** I wasn't wearing it though. If I had been things might have worked out differently.

**Dave** Rubbish! You believe what you like, but I'm sticking to my theory that life's what you make it, and having lucky rabbits' feet, plastic pigs or Egyptian beetles isn't going to make the slightest bit of difference to whether I get married, make a million or get the job of my dreams.

**Sarah** You do that!

## New Words and Expressions

| | | | |
|---|---|---|---|
| charm | /tʃɑːm/ | *n.* | 护身符 a small decorative object believed to be able to keep away evil or bring good luck to the person who wears it |
| souvenir | /ˌsuːvəˈnɪə(r)/ | *n.* | 纪念品 something you keep to remind yourself of an interesting trip, place, event, etc. |
| tenner | /ˈtenə(r)/ | *n.* | 十英镑纸币 a 10-pound paper note |
| gullible | /ˈɡʌləbl/ | *adj.* | 易受骗的，轻信的 being easily tricked or cheated, too willing to believe what other people say |
| racket | /ˈrækɪt/ | *n.* | 诈骗，骗局 a dishonest or illegal activity in making money |
| scarab | /ˈskærəb/ | *n.* | 圣甲虫形护身符 a small stone carved into the shape of a beetle |
| brooch | /brəʊtʃ/ | *n.* | 胸针 a small decorative item with a pin at the back fastened on women's clothes |
| rubbish | /ˈrʌbɪʃ/ | *n.* | 废话 nonsense |
| How come …? | | | ……怎么会的? an informal way to express surprise, meaning "How can it be that …?" |
| mumbo jumbo | /ˈmʌmbəʊ ˈdʒʌmbəʊ/ | | 莫名其妙的话 meaningless or pretentious language, usually designed to obscure an issue, confuse a listener, or the like |

## Language and Culture Notes

1. ***Background Information*** Lucky charms have been popular in various cultures since ancient

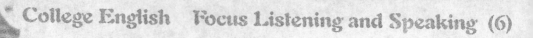

times. Wearing lucky charms may have originated from early religious beliefs or traditions but it has become part of the customs of a nation or a personal habit of an individual. Lucky charms are believed to have the supernatural power of bringing people good fortune and of protecting them from evil and misfortune. A charm can be almost any object, from a lucky shirt to a valuable gemstone, if its owner thinks it has a special significance. The materials to make lucky charms also vary, from valuable substances like precious stone, jade, pearl, ivory to ordinary stuff like shell, bone, bird feather, wood, glass, plastics, etc. To make it attractive and decorative, it is often fashioned into different shapes — round, square, oval, or shapes of an animal, fish, bird, or an insect.

2. ***... it doesn't seem to be working so far*** ... so far the lucky charm doesn't seem to have brought me any good luck
3. ***That's about it.*** That's all the good fortune (referring to the tenner she won on the lottery) the charm has brought me and nothing more.
4. ***gullible tourists*** Tourists being new to the place they are visiting, are considered to be easily persuaded to buy souvenirs of all kinds, often at prices that far exceed their real value.
5. ***You should have seen the state she got into over it***. You should have seen how very distressed the Japanese girl was when she dropped the cat statue on the ground and the cat's arm came off. To her, it was an ill omen that something disastrous might happen to her.
6. ***rabbit's feet*** In American folklore, a rabbit's foot is a charm worn around the neck to bring people good luck and ward off evil.

## Exercise 1

**Listen to the conversation carefully. Then choose the right answer to each question you hear.**

1. What seems to be the focus of the discussion?
   a. Lucky charms in different cultures.
   b. The magic powers of lucky charms.
   c. The reasons why people in different cultures have their own lucky charms.
   d. How lucky charms of different cultures came into existence.

2. Which of the following lucky charms means different things in different countries according to Sarah, Mary and Bob?
   a. The scarab.
   b. The eye pattern in a peacock feather.

c. The beetle.

d. The dragon.

3. Why does Sarah know so much about lucky charms?

   a. She has taken a course in lucky charms at university.

   b. She is an avid lucky charm collector.

   c. She is fascinated by things like lucky charms.

   d. She believes firmly in the power of lucky charms.

4. Why did the Japanese girl feel so bad?

   a. Because somebody destroyed her lucky charm.

   b. Because her lucky charm ceased to work wonders for her.

   c. Because she forgot to wear her cat statue that day.

   d. Because she dropped her cat statue and its arm came off.

5. What can you infer from the discussion?

   a. Lucky charms are nothing but superstitions.

   b. Lucky charms have little to do with what people can achieve.

   c. Wearing lucky charms has been an ancient custom in many places of the world.

   d. Lucky charms make our life more meaningful.

## Exercise 2

**Listen to the conversation again and fill in the following chart about each of the charms discussed in the discussion.**

| What is the lucky charm? | What is its supposed magic? | Who believe(s) in its magic power? |
|---|---|---|
| The horn. | It *brings good luck*. | People in *Italy*. |
| The scarab. | It *protects people from death*. | People in *Egypt*. |
| The *peacock* feather. | It *keeps evil away*; its eye pattern *protects people from the evil eye and bad luck*. | People in *India* and *Turky*. |
| A little cat statue. | Its raised arm *attracts good luck*. | A Japanese girl. |
| A *dragon* brooch. | It protects people against *unhappiness and the loss of love*. | A Chinese friend of Mary's. |

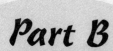

# Part B Speaking Activities

## 1. Pair Work

*Read the following quotations on luck. Then work in pairs and answer the questions orally.*

**Quotations on Luck**

1) Luck is what happens when preparation meets opportunity. (Seneca, Roman philosopher, mid-1st century AD)
2) Nature creates ability; luck provides it with opportunity. (Francois de la Rochefoucauld, French classic author 1613–1680)
3) Luck never gives, it only lends. (Swedish proverb)
4) Luck has a peculiar habit of favoring those who don't depend on it. (Anonymous)
5) Luck is the idol of the idle. (Proverb)
6) The day you decide to do it is your lucky day. (Japanese proverb)
7) The only sure thing about luck is that it will change. (Bret Harte, American writer, 1836–1902)
8) Name the greatest of all inventors. Accident. (Mark Twain)
9) Luck is when opportunity knocks and you answer. (Author unknown)
10) Each misfortune you encounter will carry in it the seed of tomorrow's good luck. (OgMandino, Italian author, 1923–1996)
11) The only good luck many great men ever had was being born with the ability and determination to overcome bad luck. (Channing Pollock, American playwright, 1880–1946)
12) When a man has no reason to trust himself, he trusts in luck. (Edgar Watson Howe, American author and editor, 1853–1937)
13) When good luck knocks at the door, let him in and keep him there. (Cervantes, Spanish novelist, 1547–1616)
14) Do not rely on a rabbit's foot for luck, after all, it did not work out so well with the rabbit. (Similar quotes)

**Questions:**

1) Which quotation do you think best illustrates luck?
2) Do you believe in luck? Why or why not?

3) Do you have a lucky charm? If yes, what is it? Does it work?
4) Do you do anything for good luck before an important exam or interview? Has it worked?
5) Do you believe that certain objects, numbers or actions can bring people either good or bad luck?
6) Do you agree with Dave that we make our own luck in this world? Why or why not?

## 2. Communicative Function: Discussing Fortune and Misfortune

In life we all have our share of good and bad luck, or fortune and misfortune. Although some instances of fortune and misfortune are attributable to our own actions and choices, but sometimes they seem to occur randomly. While we may not know why we become the recipients of a lottery win or a life-long illness, we need to learn how to deal with whatever fortune or misfortune life throws our way. Have you had an event of fortune or misfortune happen to you that changed your life in some way? What have you learned from the experience? What do you think is the right attitude toward good fortune and misfortune in life? How do you think we should handle misfortune and make the best of a bad situation? In the box below, you'll find some sentences and structures that you may find useful when discussing fortune and misfortune.

### DISCUSSING FORTUNE AND MISFORTUNE

It was a piece of sheer good luck / bad luck.
I lucked into / onto / upon a great job.
I seem to have nothing but bad / ill / tough / no luck.
It was just my luck / I'm down on my luck / in / out of luck.
He pushed / crowded his luck and ended up a loser.
As luck would have it, he missed the final goal when he jumped.
Don't give up. You never know your luck.
It was a(n) wonderful / thrilling / exciting / heartening / educational / life-changing / humbling / frustrating / painful / traumatic / heart-breaking experience for me.
That experience changed my life and helped me mature as a person / taught me self-reliance and independence / inspired me to follow my dreams / gave me the opportunity to learn more about myself / helped me realize what is really

important in life.
Looking back, I realize now that the accident was a blessing in disguise.
Without that chance meeting, I could have never had my dream come true.
Some people waste opportunities that come their way while others are able to find opportunities in the worst situations.
When faced with misfortune, some people despair and let it defeat them while others rise to the challenge and manage to not only survive but also thrive.
When misfortune befalls us / strikes, we may feel bewildered, disappointed, upset and even angry / we are tempted to wallow in self-pity and give up hope / we often lose heart and allow bitterness and pain to take over.
I admire those who bear misfortune with dignity and grace / who face life's challenges with courage / who persevere against all odds and never give up.
How we deal with / respond to misfortune is the true test of character / can make the difference between defeat and victory in our lives.
Misfortune and adversity are part of the human experience.
Hardship educates a person and pushes him to do better and achieve more.
We have to be brave in the face of misfortune / strive to overcome adversity and turn it to advantage.
When faced with misfortune and adversity, it is important that we do not lose hope / that we keep a positive mindset / that we remember there are people who are worse off than us / that we get support from family and friends.

## *A Model*

**Bob** Dave, you know what? I read a story in the newspaper about a man who won one million dollars in the lottery.

**Dave** What good luck! I wish I could be so lucky. These days I seem to have nothing but bad luck.

**Bob** Well, you wouldn't feel so sorry for yourself when you hear what happened to the lucky man.

**Dave** What misfortune could happen to him with one million dollars in his possession?

**Bob** Well, after winning the money, he quit his job, bought houses and cars for himself and his family, and started his own company. But he's not the business type. In a few years, his company went bankrupt. Now he has lost all his money and his wife has also left him. He

says he wishes he had never won the lottery.

**Dave** Well, well. That's too bad.

**Bob** This is yet another story of good fortune turned sour. Actually many lottery winners have sad endings. You know this really makes me think. It seems that the line between good fortune and misfortune is not always so clear-cut. What appears to be fortune may lead to misfortune and what appears to be misfortune may lead to fortune.

**Dave** You're right. I have a friend who was paralyzed from the neck down in a car accident right after graduation from college. After a period of depression and despair, he decided to stop feeling sorry for himself and do something with his life. He had always been interested in literature, so he decided to take to writing. Now he is a columnist for several newspapers and magazines. He has also started a website to help people with handicaps. He told me that he has found the true meaning of life and is actually enjoying life more than before the accident.

**Bob** That's inspiring. I always admire people who have the courage to face up to life's challenges and achieve great things.

**Dave** I wish that accident had never happened to my friend. But I think his story shows that misfortune doesn't have to stop us from having a happy and meaningful life. In the face of misfortune, it's easy to despair and lose hope. But if you keep a positive attitude and don't give up, you can turn tragedy into triumph.

**Bob** True. So whether it is fortune or misfortune, it is really our attitude that makes all the difference.

**Dave** You're right. Sometimes life seems beyond our control. But the decision we make to deal with misfortune is perhaps what really counts in the end.

**Bob** Exactly.

*Now try to use what you've learned in this lesson and carry out the following tasks.*

1) Work in pairs. Take turns to describe an event of good or bad luck that has happened to you. In what way has it changed you or your life?
2) Form groups of three or four. Discuss how differently people may respond to fortune and misfortune. What do you think is the right attitude toward fortune and misfortune? Mark Twain once said, "No misfortune can withstand the assault of laughter." Do you agree? What else do you think can help us deal with misfortune?

# Part C Listen and Relax

## A Song

**Listen to the song *Sailing* and sing along.**

### *Sailing*

*I am sailing, I am sailing,*
*Home again 'cross the sea.*
*I am sailing, stormy waters,*
*To be near you, to be free.*

*I am flying, I am flying,*
*Like a bird 'cross the sky.*
*I am flying, passing high clouds,*
*To be near you, to be free.*

*Can you hear me, can you hear me,*
*Thro' the dark night far away?*
*I am dying, forever trying,*
*To be with you, who can say.*

*We are sailing, we are sailing,*
*Home again 'cross the sea.*
*We are sailing stormy waters,*
*To be near you, to be free.*
*Oh Lord, to be near you, to be free.*
*Oh Lord, to be near you, to be free.*
*Oh Lord.*

**Notes**

1. *The song was performed by the British singer and song writer Rod Stewart (1945– ).*
2. ***'cross*** across
3. ***thro'*** through

# Part D Further Listening

## Conversation 1

### It Means Good Luck

**Exercise**

**Listen to the conversation and choose the right answer to each question you hear.**

**Allison** Hi, Linda. How's your piano practicing going?

**Linda** Oh, pretty good. I think I'm almost ready for my recital next week.

**Allison** Well, break a leg!

**Linda** What? Why would I want to do that?

**Allison** It's just an expression, Linda. It means good luck!

**Linda** Really? Then I hope you break your legs, too, on your test later.

**Allison** No, just say, "Break a leg." Otherwise, it sounds like you really want the other person to have an accident or something.

**Linda** English is so confusing sometimes.

**Allison** By the way, that's a nice necklace you're wearing.

**Linda** Thanks. It's my lucky necklace. I always wear it when I perform.

**Allison** Why? Does it help you play better?

**Linda** Not really. But I just feel more comfortable with it on.

**Allison** I understand. I used to have a lucky rabbit's foot.

**Linda** A rabbit's foot? Why is that good luck?

**Allison** Long ago, rabbits were believed to be magical since they lived under the ground. People thought they could talk with spirits down there.

**Linda** I'm so surprised you believe in something like a rabbit's foot, Allison.

**Allison** Why?

**Linda** I always thought Westerners were very scientific in their thinking and didn't believe in those kinds of things.

**Allison** I don't really. It's just for fun. And neither do most other Westerners. But some do believe in things like good luck charms and horoscopes.

**Linda** So even you people can be sort of superstitious.

**Allison** That's for sure. And despite how "scientific" we all are now, certain ideas about what brings good or bad luck continue to exist.

1. Which of the following expressions means good luck?
   a. Break your leg.
   b. Break a leg.
   c. Break your legs.
   d. Break a leg of yours.

2. Why does Linda wear her lucky necklace when she performs?
   a. She feels better with a necklace on.
   b. She performs better with her lucky necklace on.
   c. She feels more comfortable with her lucky necklace on.
   d. She feels she is more beautiful wearing her favorite necklace.

3. What do you know about Linda?
   a. She speaks good English.
   b. She's a good pianist.
   c. She's rather superstitious.
   d. She believes rabbits are magical.

4. Which of the following is true?
   a. Westerners are very scientific in their thinking.
   b. Most people in the West believe in luck.
   c. Linda and Allison don't really believe in luck.
   d. Linda doesn't believe in lucky charms but Allison does.

## Conversation 2

# Could You Tell Me More About It?

### Exercise

**Listen to the conversation and write down your answers to the following questions.**

**Allison** Hello, Linda.

**Linda** Hello.

**Allison** How are you doing?

**Linda** Nothing much. I just stay home the whole day and think about things we talked last week.

**Allison** What bothers you, Linda?

**Linda** I was just thinking about what is considered good luck or bad luck, something like that. Oh, Allison. Could you tell me more about it?

**Allison** Do you know a kind of leaf called clover? It's a small plant. Then a four-leaf clover is considered lucky.

**Linda** How come?

**Allison** Because it's unusual. Most clovers have only three leaves.

**Linda** Oh, so you're lucky to even find one.

**Allison** Right! On the other hand, breaking a mirror is considered bad luck.

**Linda** Why?

**Allison** Because a mirror holds a reflection of you. What happens to that reflection also happens to you.

**Linda** I see.

**Allison** There are many other beliefs like these. But often no one knows for sure where these beliefs come from.

**Linda** In the Chinese culture, some things are considered lucky because they're puns for other "lucky" words.

**Allison** What do you mean?

**Linda** For example, the Chinese word for "orange" is "ji". The word for "luck" is also "ji".

**Allison** So oranges are "lucky" fruit.

**Linda** Exactly. Another lucky fruit is the pineapple. Its name sounds like "fortune comes". And the number "six" is fortunate for similar reasons.

**Allison** So do many Chinese superstitions have to do with getting rich?

**Linda** You said it. Luck and fortune go hand in hand, you know.

**Allison** Sometimes I feel like I can use all the luck I can get.

**Linda** I know. That's probably why people still have superstitions.

**Allison** Well, they're interesting to learn about. But I try not to take those beliefs too seriously.

**Linda** Same here.

**Allison** Oh, watch out! You almost stepped on a crack in the sidewalk!

**Linda** So?

**Allison** Stepping on cracks is bad luck. "Step on a crack, break your mother's back."

**Linda** I think maybe you're the one who's cracked.

1. Why is breaking a mirror considered bad luck according to Allison?
   *Because a mirror holds a reflection of you. What happens to that reflection also happens to you.*
2. What fruits are believed to be lucky fruits in Chinese culture? Why?
   *Orange and pineapple. Because the Chinese word for "orange" and the word for "luck" sound the same. Similarly, the Chinese words for pineapple sound like "fortune comes".*
3. Why do many Chinese superstitions have much to do with getting rich?
   *Because luck and fortune often go hand in hand.*

# Part E Home Listening

## A Story

### Beginner's Luck (Part I)

#### Exercise

**Listen to the first half of the story and choose the right answer to each question you hear after the story.**

James Milner had always been an average boy. At school he had never done very well, but he hadn't done very badly either. When it came to the end of the year, he always just passed his exams, though he never got great marks.

After he left school, he had gone to an average university, not a very good one, but not a bad

one either. He had studied economics and commerce there, and got a degree. James didn't really want to be a great businessman, a fantastic entrepreneur, an accountant or even a politician, even though his father pushed him a lot. James Milner came from quite a wealthy family, and he had always felt the pressure of his father's expectations breathing down his neck. James didn't really want to do very much at all in life really. He liked to take it easy, sleep a lot, and to travel. His father, however, had great expectations for his son.

James worked in a fast food restaurant for a while after he left university. It was OK there. No, the money wasn't great, but his colleagues were friendly, and the work wasn't difficult, even though the shifts were terrible. James hated working late at night or early in the morning. He really just wanted to sleep. And to travel, to go to other places. The problem was that James was too lazy to travel. He had never actually ever been further than Brighton, about an hour from where he was born and lived. Still he liked the idea of travel.

After a year, James' father was desperate. "You must do something with your life, James!" he said. And so he telephoned his brother, James' uncle. James' uncle was the head of a very important bank in the city of London.

Next Monday James was sitting there in front of a computer which he had no idea how to use, apparently controlling the financial fortunes of Western Europe. His hands were shaking as he sat down at his desk and put on the telephone headset by the side of his desk. "At least if I put this on I'll look like I know what I'm doing," he thought. Then he stared at the computer screen in front of him with the mysterious programme. There were hundreds of numbers and dates and names of cities written on it, as well as lots of strange names like "NYSE" and "CAC40" and other things. He had no idea what any of it meant.

When he put the telephone headset on here he didn't hear orders for extra french fries and different types of hamburgers, but excited men in faraway places shouting orders at him like "2000 Tokyo heavy! Sell! Sell!! Sell!!!" or "Coming up on NYSE! Buy! Buy!! Buy!!!" At first he sat there and tried to pretend he knew what he was doing. He tried pressing a few keys on the computer in front of him, but nothing seemed to happen to the screen. Lots of numbers appeared, frequently. Then they disappeared.

1. Which of the following best describes James?
   a. Ambitious.
   b. Intelligent.
   c. Neither intelligent nor stupid.
   d. Both intelligent and ambitious.

2. What did James want to do with his life?
   a. To be successful in business.
   b. To become a fantastic entrepreneur.

c. To travel around the world.

d. To take it easy and not do much.

3. What do you know about James' father?

a. He was the head of an important bank in the City of London.

b. He gave James a lot of pressure.

c. He owned a fast food restaurant chain.

d. He came from a wealthy family.

4. What seemed to be James' job at the bank?

a. Buying and selling stocks and shares for his clients.

b. Doing financial analysis.

c. Controlling the fortunes of Asia and Western Europe.

d. Taking over other banks.

## A Story

# Beginner's Luck (Part II)

### Exercise

**Listen to the second half of the story and choose the right answer for each question you hear after the story.**

Even though he was worried at first, James soon learned how to use the computer and how to do his new job. It wasn't that difficult after all, he soon learned. The people around him weren't all that intelligent or clever, he realised. He even thought that it wasn't really that different to working in the fast food restaurant. Instructions came through either on his telephone headset or on his computer screen and he followed them — when he understood them. Mostly the work consisted of buying and selling things. It was like a market. Instead of stocks and shares and personal fortunes, James imagined that he was selling carrots and cabbages and cauliflowers. When he had to make his own decisions, James took a coin out of his pocket, threw it up in the air, and depending on which side it landed on, he bought or sold.

It was amazing, he couldn't believe it, but he started to be successful. After two weeks on the job, one of his bosses came up to him and said "Great work, James!" James didn't even know what he had done. He just kept on doing the same thing, buying or selling when he felt like it. "Beginner's luck!" laughed his friend Davy next to him, every time that James seemed to manage to earn or save

a fortune just by clicking the right keys on his computer.

James began to get more courageous. He put bigger and bigger numbers into his computer. Bigger numbers seemed to create even bigger numbers. It was great fun, he thought. The bigger the number, the bigger the reward. Buy 1,000 shares! Sell 100,000! Buy a million, then sell them again ten minutes later.

Then his boss came to his desk holding a huge bottle of vintage champagne. "This is for you, James! Great work on the Singapore bank takeover there! We were risking a lot, but I was following you and I could see that you knew exactly what you were doing! You kept cool throughout it all!"

James and Davy and the boss opened the champagne right there and drank it all. Some of it spilled on his computer, but he didn't care. He felt great! After drinking all the champagne they all went to a bar and carried on drinking some more. It was nearly two o'clock in the morning when the bar closed. Davy said that he was going back into the office — seeing as he was still awake he thought he could get some work done on the Asian markets. James was still so happy he went into the office as well. He was so tired he couldn't see what he was doing, but he just kept on shouting "buy" or "sell" and pushing all the buttons on his computer.

Sometime the next day James woke up feeling very bad. It was time to take a break, he thought. After phoning up his boss and telling him that he wouldn't be in for a few days, James bought a ticket to Thailand.

Two days later, James was sitting on a beach in Thailand. He felt great, he felt fantastic. This was what he had always wanted. Later that evening he went into town to find a bar. He noticed that there was a small stand selling English-language newspapers. Something about the headline on the *International Herald Tribune* made him stop. Wait a second, he thought, that's the name of my bank. He picked up the newspaper and started to read the article. At first he didn't really understand what was happening. But it didn't take long for him to understand. He didn't bother buying the newspaper, but walked off and found a bar quickly.

In the bar there were some other Westerners, talking in English. "Have you heard about this bank that's collapsed?" they were saying. "It looks like the entire London Stock Exchange might collapse!!!" "It's incredible!" said one of the other people. "Some idiot sold 100,000 shares for 10p each, instead of buying 10 for 100,000 pounds! And that was only one of the mistakes he made ..."

James left the bar immediately and went to the nearest cash machine. He took all the money that he could from the cash machine. Then he went back to the bar and asked if they needed a new barman. "I've got lots of experience! I used to work in a fast food restaurant in London!" he told the owner, who offered him a job immediately.

"By the way," said James, "My name's Fernando ... just in case anyone ever comes looking for me ..."

1. What did he do when he had to make a decision whether to buy or sell?
   a. He would consult his boss as to what to do.

b. He would depend on his luck to decide it for him.

c. He would ask Dave to help him.

d. He would use his experience at the fast food restaurant to guide him.

2. How come James became so successful at his job in a short time?

a. He learned to do his work very fast.

b. He had a special talent with numbers.

c. He was a born businessman.

d. He had what is called "beginner's luck".

3. What happened to the bank in the end?

a. It collapsed.

b. It merged with another bank.

c. It took over a bank in Singapore.

d. It caused the entire London Stock Exchange to collapse.

4. What can you infer from the story?

a. James escaped punishment by flying to Thailand.

b. James should not be held responsible for what he had done.

c. James was guilty of toppling over his bank.

d. James' luck finally deserted him.

# Test 1

## Part A

**In this part you'll hear 8 short conversations. At the end of each conversation a question will be asked about what was said. Both the conversation and the question will be read only once. Listen carefully and choose the right answer to each question you hear.** *(8 points)*

1. **W** How do you feel about flying?

   **M** Frankly I don't mind flying. What I don't like is not being able to keep an eye on my luggage. Whenever the man at the airport takes it away I never expect to see it again.

   **Q.** What is the man worried about?

   a. His own safety.

   b. His own luggage.

   c. Losing his luggage.

   d. Who takes away his luggage.

2. **W** What do you think of your new boss, John?

   **M** Well, he is full of praise when you do well. But when you make a mistake, you'd better watch out.

   **Q.** What can you learn about John's boss?

   a. He has a terrible temper.

   b. He thinks John is his best worker.

   c. He gets very angry when John makes a mistake.

   d. He is sincere.

3. **W** Well, you said you didn't care very much for your job. Have you ever thought about quitting?

   **M** Not really. You see I have a lot of friends in the office. I'm part of the family. Quitting would be like getting a divorce.

**Q.** Why doesn't the man want to leave his present job?

a. He has good relations with his boss.

b. He doesn't want to part with his friends in the office.

c. He has got a large family to support.

d. He's getting a divorce.

4. **M** How are you, Judy? I do hope you're free next Saturday. We're having a party to celebrate our second wedding anniversary. You will be able to come, won't you?

**W** I'd love to come, but it's my mother's birthday. And she'd be terribly disappointed if I didn't spend the weekend at home. I'm sorry.

**Q.** Where will the woman go next Saturday?

a. To a restaurant for a birthday party.

b. Back home.

c. To the wedding anniversary.

d. To the party.

5. **M** I almost had an accident. I was crossing the street just now and was almost hit by a car. Fortunately I jumped back in time.

**W** How awful! You should have got the license number of that car so you could report the driver to the police department.

**Q.** What does the woman mean?

a. The man should report to the police about the accident.

b. The man should try to recall the license number of the car.

c. The man would not be able to report the driver to the police.

d. The man should have been careful while crossing the street.

6. **W** Jack, would you please read this letter of application I've just written? I'd like to have your opinion.

**M** If I were you, I'd change the beginning. Write about your education first and include much more information about your work experience. And it's good to say something about your family, too.

**Q.** What can we conclude from the conversation?

a. The letter may have to be rewritten.

b. The man must be a career advisor.

c. The woman is a modest person.

d. The woman does not have much education.

7. **M** Where can we find a school for stubborn children with bad manners? Tom won't listen to anyone now.
   **W** I don't think he's stubborn. He's independent, you know. But don't worry. I'll look for a school for creative children.
   **Q.** What can we conclude from the conversation?
   a. It's hard to find a suitable school for children nowadays.
   b. There is always some gap between generations.
   c. Tom is stubborn sometimes, but he's also quite creative.
   d. Tom seems to be a difficult child but he is actually quite independent.

8. **M** I suppose the big red London buses are even more famous than the tube trains. Visitors can see London from the upstairs windows.
   **W** Old people usually ride downstairs while younger people especially visitors like riding upstairs. It's certainly the cheapest way to see the most interesting things in London.
   **Q.** What are they talking about?
   a. Advantages of riding in London's big red buses.
   b. Public transportation in London.
   c. The cheapest way to tour London.
   d. The most interesting things in London.

## Part B

**You'll hear two longer conversations. Each will be read only once. Listen carefully and choose the right answer to each question you hear.** *(7 points)*

**Conversation 1**

**M** Hi, Jane. How are you doing these days?
**W** Nothing much. And how are you?
**M** Fine. Jane, I'd like to discuss something with you. Do you have a minute?
**W** Sure. I've just got out of my eleven o'clock class. I don't have another class until this afternoon.
**M** Good. Listen. I've just received an e-mail from the computer center. They are looking for students to help with the work of the school website this summer. They need two assistants. They asked me if I knew anyone that might be interested. I thought you might like to consider the job.

**W** Sounds like fun. I can type pretty fast, but I don't have a lot of experience.

**M** Well, I don't think any experience or knowledge is necessary. And with your interests in computers and the Internet, I think you would be good for the job. Also they're paying good money. What do you think?

**W** It sounds like a great chance to get some experience. Thanks for thinking of me.

*Questions 1 to 3 are based on the conversation you've just heard.*

1. What's the probable relationship between the two speakers?
   a. Student and teacher.
   b. Roommates.
   c. Both working as assistants at the computer center.
   d. Friends.

2. What does the man tell the woman?
   a. About a new school website.
   b. About the job requirements of the school website.
   c. About a job opportunity for the school website.
   d. About the experience needed to apply for the school website job.

3. What can you infer from the conversation?
   a. The woman is going to take the job.
   b. The woman has worked as a typist before.
   c. The man likes the job because he needs the money.
   d. The man has much working experience in computer.

**Conversation 2**

**Interviewer** Hi, Mr Blake, could you tell us something about the economic forecasts for next year, for example, what will happen to housing costs?

**Mr Blake** Well, there's good news for buyers. Prices won't increase. In fact, they'll fall slightly. There are different reasons for this. First, which seems to be the main reason, is that it won't be so easy to borrow money, you know. The other reason is that there are still a lot of empty new houses on the market.

**Interviewer** I see. And what about food prices? Will they fall too?

**Mr Blake** I'm afraid not. You see, inflation will increase, so consumer prices will rise too. I think we can expect a 3% rise in prices.

**Interviewer** Some economists say that unemployment will rise. Are you one of these people?

**Mr Blake** No, I'm not. I'm sure it'll decrease. Trade with other countries has improved

dramatically over the past year. And the increase demand for goods means that there will be more jobs.

**Interviewer** Well, if unemployment falls, can we expect wages to fall, too?

**Mr Blake** No, no, the average wage will increase. Not very much, I'm afraid, but there will be a slight increase.

**Interviewer** One financial question, Mr Blake. What will happen to petrol prices? Will they increase or decrease next year?

**Mr Blake** That's a very difficult question to answer because we don't know what'll happen in the oil producing countries. I have a feeling that prices will go down. However, I could be wrong!

**Interviewer** Mr Blake, thank you very much for your time.

**Mr Blake** Thank you.

*Questions 4 to 7 are based on the conversation you've just heard.*

4. Who might be Mr Blake?
   a. <u>An economist.</u>
   b. An expert in international trade.
   c. A real estate agent.
   d. A forecaster.

5. What is the main reason for a slight fall in housing costs according to Mr Blake?
   a. The housing market is not looking good.
   b. Banks are encouraging buyers to get a loan.
   c. There are a lot of empty new houses on the market.
   d. <u>Money won't be easy to borrow.</u>

6. What is Mr Blake's opinion on unemployment?
   a. It will surely rise.
   b. <u>It will surely go down.</u>
   c. It will rise soon.
   d. It will go down soon.

7. How does Mr Blake answer the interview's question about petrol prices next year?
   a. He finds it too hard to answer.
   b. He says he is not sure if the prices will decrease.
   c. <u>He says that the prices will decrease but he is not sure.</u>
   d. He can't give a correct answer.

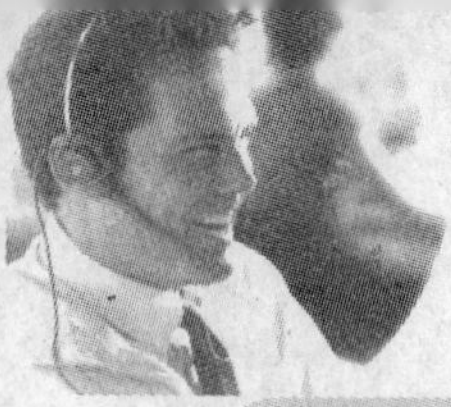



## Part C

**In this part you'll hear a passage three times. When it is read for the first time, you should listen carefully for its general idea. Then listen to the passage for the second time and fill in the blanks numbered 1 to 7 with the exact words you've just heard. For blanks numbered 8 to 10, fill in the missing information. You can either use the exact words you've just heard or write down the main points in your own words. Finally, check your answers when the passage is read for the third time.** *(10 points)*

Parents' attitude towards their children 1) *indicates* cultural values. In the United States, it is common for parents to put the 2) *newborn* in a 3) *separate* room that belongs to it only. On the one hand, this helps to 4) *preserve* the parents' privacy, a highly 5) *cherished* value there; and on the other hand, it allows the child to get accustomed to having his or her own room, which is seen as a first step towards independence.

American parents believe that making money at an early age helps children appreciate its value, learn to 6) *budget*, and prepare themselves for future 7) *financial* independence. From an early age, the American child is encouraged to make up his own mind. 8) *He is made to believe that he himself is the best judge of what he wants and what he should do*. It is nothing unusual that children work for money in or outside their homes. This is looked upon as a first step to foster autonomy.

Interestingly enough, 9) *American parents firmly refuse to let their children enter the adult world though helping them to act somewhat like adults*. If the parents are about to entertain guests at home, they put the children early to bed. For them their business or social activities are their private reserve and children are allowed to be present only when the invitation is extended to children. When they go to parties, they often leave the children with babysitters. 10) *This again shows the importance they attach to privacy*.

## Part D

**In this part you'll hear three short passages. Each will be read only once. After each passage, you'll be asked some questions about what was said. Listen carefully and choose the right answer to each question you hear.** *(15 points)*

**Passage 1**

Every culture in the world believes certain superstitions. Even societies that are very rational and scientific are sometimes a little bit superstitious. For example, the United States is a country that is very advanced in science and technology. But even in American society, people sometimes believe superstitions. Americans consider "thirteen" an unlucky number. So it is rare to find a building with a thirteenth floor in the States. There is always a twelfth and a fourteenth floor, but there is rarely a thirteenth floor. Many people believe that if you live or work on the thirteenth floor of a building, you will have bad luck. Some people in the States also believe that if Friday falls on the thirteenth day of the month, they will have bad luck.

Some Americans believe they will have bad luck if they walk under a ladder. Even if people say they are not superstitious, they will often avoid walking under a ladder. Often, people consider it unlucky to break a mirror. If a person breaks a mirror, he or she will have seven years of sad misfortune.

Americans also think they will have bad luck if a black cat crosses their path. A long time ago, people believed that black cats were really witches in disguise. However, some things are thought to bring good luck. For example, some Americans believe if they carry a rabbit's foot, they will have good luck. Some people believe they will have good luck if they find a four-leaf clover. Others think they will have good luck if they find a penny on the ground and pick it up.

All in all, even if a society becomes very advanced in science and technology, people will always remain a little bit superstitious.

*Questions 1 to 3 are based on the passage you've just heard.*

1. What is the main idea of the passage?
   a. People everywhere in the world are superstitious.
   b. In the United States most people are still superstitious.
   c. Even in scientifically advanced countries, superstitions still exist.
   d. People should not be too superstitious.

2. What do some Americans believe?
   a. Walking under a ladder will bring them good luck.
   b. Walking under a ladder will bring them bad luck.
   c. Black cats are dangerous.
   d. Rabbits can bring people good luck.

3. What is implied in the passage?
   a. When societies become more advanced in science and technology, superstitions will be eliminated.
   b. Superstitions will die out sooner or later.

c. With the development of science and technology, people will become less superstitious.

d. Superstitions are quite harmless.

**Passage 2**

Human life cannot continue without science and technology. For many years human society develops with the advance of science and technology, and the development of science and technology in turn brings progress to mankind. Because of this, the life we are living now is more civilized than that of our forefathers.

The development of science and technology has brought about many changes in people's life. For example, the inventions of TV and space rockets have opened a new era for mankind. Through the use of TV people can hear the sound and learn the events which actually happen thousands of miles away. Owing to the invention of spaceships, we have realized our dream to land on the moon, which was impossible in the past.

Science and technology also play an important role in the construction of our country. It is hard to imagine that the modernization of industry, agriculture and national defense of our country can be realized without the application of modern science and technology. In a sense, we may say the construction of our country is just like building a skyscraper, and science and technology are its base. Without the base, the skyscraper can't be built.

In a word, we should all try our best to contribute, however small, to the development of science and technology so as to provide a more solid base on which to build our country.

*Questions 4 to 6 are based on the passage you've just heard.*

4. What is the passage mainly about?
   a. The importance of developing science and technology.
   b. The application of science and technology in the construction of industry, agriculture and national defense.
   c. The important roles science and technology play in our society.
   d. The relationship between the development of science and technology and human life.

5. Why is the life we're living now more civilized than that of our forefathers?
   a. Because we have better manners than our forefathers.
   b. Because we enjoy more material comforts than our forefathers did.
   c. Because the development of science and technology has enabled our society to make progress.
   d. Because our life is changing all the time with the development of science and technology.

6. Which of the following opened a new era for mankind according to the passage?
   a. The inventions of rockets and robots.

b. The inventions of TV and space rockets.

c. The landing on the moon.

d. The building of skyscrapers.

**Passage 3**

Doctors, along with lawyers and professors are among the best-paid professionals in the United States. Nowadays it is common for medical doctors to earn incomes of more than $200,000 a year. Specialists, particularly surgeons, might earn several times that amount.

Physicians list many reasons why they deserve to be so well rewarded for their work. One reason is the long and expensive preparation required to become a physician in the U.S. Most would-be physicians first attend college for four years, which can cost more than $30,000 annually at one of the best private institutions. Prospective physicians then attend medical school for another four years. Tuition alone can exceed $20,000 a year. By the time they have obtained their medical degrees, many young physicians are deeply in debt. They still face three to five years of residency in a hospital, the first year as an intern and apprentice physician. The hours are long and the pay is relatively low.

Doctors work long hours and must accept a great deal of responsibility. Many medical procedures, even quite routine ones, involve risk. To be a good doctor will require not only profound medical knowledge, skilled experience, cool judgment but also the strong power of enduring intense pressures. More often than not, they have to work overtime. They might be called to an emergency at any time of a day. It is understandable that doctors want to be well rewarded for making decisions which can mean the difference between life and death.

*Questions 7 to 10 are based on the passage you've just heard.*

7. What does the passage mainly tell us?

   a. The qualifications required to be a good doctor.

   b. The reasons why doctors in the U.S. are very well-paid.

   c. Heavy workload and high pay for doctors in the U.S.

   d. The medical profession is well-paid but very risky.

8. For how long can you earn a medical degree in the U.S.?

   a. Four years.

   b. Eight years.

   b. Three to five years.

   c. Ten years.

9. How much does a student at a very good medical institution need to pay for a medical degree?
   a. Over 80,000 dollars.
   b. About 100,000 dollars.
   c. Over 1600,000 dollars.
   d. About 200,000 dollars.

10. What are the qualifications of a good doctor according to the passage?
    a. Having very good medical knowledge, skilled experience and cool mind.
    b. Having extremely good medical knowledge, skilled experience, cool judgment and good health.
    c. Having very good medical knowledge, skilled experience, cool judgment and the strong power to endure great pressures.
    d. Having extremely good medical knowledge, skilled experience, cool judgment and the strength to deal with any risks.

Total Score: 35 points

# Test 2

## Part A

**In this part you'll hear 8 short conversations. At the end of each conversation a question will be asked about what was said. Both the conversation and the question will be read only once. Listen carefully and choose the right answer for each question you hear.** *(8 points)*

1. **M** I thought you were going to see your aunt in Hangzhou last weekend.
   **W** I intended to, but at the last minute she called and said the weekend was inconvenient for her so I stayed at home.
   **Q.** What did the woman do last weekend?
   a. She went to Hangzhou.
   b. She visited her aunt.
   c. She stayed at home.
   d. She called her aunt.

2. **M** I just got off the plane. My secretary told me that she had already made a room reservation for me. Which room is mine?
   **W** I'm sorry. We have no record of your reservation.
   **Q.** Where does this conversation take place?
   a. In a travel agency.
   b. In a hotel.
   c. In a hospital.
   d. At the airport.

3. **W** I hear you are going on a trip to Europe. When do you plan to leave?
   **M** My flight leaves Shanghai on the 27th of next month. However, I only plan to go to England. I don't have enough money to tour all of Europe.

Q. What is the man planning to do?

a. He's going on a tour of several foreign countries.

b. He's saving money for a trip abroad.

c. He's leaving Shanghai later this month.

d. He's going to visit one foreign country.

4. W I was half an hour late for Professor Harrison's lecture this morning. Could you lend me your notes, Jim?

M Sure. But you won't find much in my notes. Actually he didn't say anything important during your absence.

Q. What do we learn from the conversation?

a. Jim's notes are not very good.

b. Professor Harrison doesn't teach well.

c. The woman doesn't have to borrow notes from Jim.

d. The woman should have come to the lecture earlier.

5. M When will you be going on holiday with me?

W I'm not sure. You know I've just started a new job at Johnson's company. I won't get a moment free until the training period is over.

Q. Why can't the woman go on holiday with the man now?

a. She's not sure if her boss would allow her to go.

b. She's not sure if she really wants to go.

c. She's running a training class for the company.

d. She's busy with training for her new job.

6. W What are you going to major in, John?

M I think it'll either be education or medicine. My father wants me to be a teacher or a doctor, but I'd rather build skyscrapers or things like that.

Q. What does John want to be?

a. A teacher.

b. An architect.

c. A doctor.

d. A lawyer.

7. M Hey, Mary. The Uptown Theatre has "Pirates of the Caribbean". Why don't we forget about the exam and go and see it?

W Sorry, I can't. I need to brush up on my notes.

Q. What must the woman do?

<u>a. Review her notes.</u>
b. Type her notes.
c. Make notes.
d. Take notes.

8. **W** I wish Laura would call me when she knows she'll be late. This is the third time we have had to wait for her.
**M** I can't agree more, but she does have to drive through very heavy traffic to get here.
**Q.** How does the man feel about Laura's being late?
a. He's not happy with Laura.
b. He's worried about Laura.
c. He's rather angry with Laura.
<u>d. He's annoyed but quite understanding.</u>

## Part B

**You'll hear two longer conversations. Each will be read only once. Listen carefully and choose the right answer to each question you hear.** *(7 points)*

**Conversation 1**

**Tim** Hey, Nancy. My teacher asked me to write a paper in nutrition. But I don't know much about vitamins. Do you mind telling me something about them? You're a specialist in nutrition.

**Nancy** With pleasure. Vitamins are natural chemical substances that we all need in order to stay healthy.

**Tim** I know the main vitamins are Vitamin A, Vitamin B and Vitamin C.

**Nancy** Yes, Vitamin A is especially important for the eyes and the skin. It's found in many foods, mostly found in carrots, green vegetables and liver.

**Tim** What about Vitamins B and C?

**Nancy** Vitamin B is important for our mental health. In fact, our whole nervous system, including our brain, needs Vitamin B in order to work properly. The best sources of Vitamin B are beans, nuts and grains. Vitamin C is necessary for keeping our muscles healthy. It's also necessary for protecting the body's cells from dangerous substances. Vitamin C may protect us from certain viruses. Vitamin C is found in all fruits. The greatest amount of this vitamin is contained in berries such as blueberries and strawberries, and in oranges.

**Tim** Thank you, Nancy. I've learned a lot today.

*Questions 1 to 4 are based on the conversation you've just heard.*

1. Who might be the woman?
   a. A doctor.
   b. A pharmacist.
   c. A nutritionist.
   d. A specialist.

2. Why do we need to take Vitamin A according to the woman?
   a. Because it is important for the whole nervous system.
   b. Because it is important for the eyes and the skin.
   c. Because it can help our brain to work properly.
   d. Because it can help protect our body cells from dangerous substances.

3. What are the best sources of Vitamin B?
   a. Beans, carrots and liver.
   b. Nuts, beans and grains.
   c. Nuts, berries and beans.
   d. Beans, nuts and carrots.

4. What can Vitamin C do?
   a. It can help us develop healthy body cells.
   b. It can help us develop strong muscles.
   c. It can protect us from certain viruses.
   d. It can protect our muscles from dangerous substances.

**Conversation 2**

**W** Dr Stone, many experts see family meetings as an ideal opportunity to open the doors of communication between parents and children. But how do you go about holding a meeting?

**M** In my opinion family meetings should be handled around the kitchen table instead of the boardroom table. They should be held weekly, at a regular time that everyone agrees on. Meetings should be short and never an unhappy experience. People can express things that are bothering them, but should never attack others. It's not a fighting time. It's a time when everyone gets to talk and has an opinion.

**W** Should young kids be included for family meetings?

**M** Sure. Kids of all ages have a lot to gain from such meetings. They learn how to speak up in meetings and their opinion means something. They learn the democratic process and are more likely to take responsibility for the decision being made. If they're a part of the decision making process then they are more likely to follow through. So if it comes to household chores then the child is more likely to do them if they've had a chance to say yes or no, or a chance to say what they like to do.

**W** Then why do some people fail at family meetings?

**M** Many people have failed at family meetings because they always focus on what's wrong. The most successful ones offer compliments to each other and acknowledge ways someone has contributed.

**W** Can you summarize the value of family meetings, Dr Stone?

**M** Overall, family meetings can strengthen the bonds between children and parents. They are the most important meetings of our life.

**W** Thank you very much.

*Questions 5 to 7 are based on the conversation you've just heard.*

5. Which of the following is true of family meetings?
   a. They should be short but formal.
   b. They should be held at meal time in the kitchen.
   <u>c. They should be a happy experience.</u>
   d. They should be held whenever problems arise in the family.

6. Why do some people fail at family meetings?
   a. Because they often focus on the mistakes of other family members.
   b. Because they don't see their own shortcomings.
   c. Because they offer too many compliments to each other.
   <u>d. Because they give their full attention to what has gone wrong.</u>

7. What can we learn from the conversation?
   a. Family meetings can improve the relations among family members.
   <u>b. Family meetings can bring parents and their children much closer.</u>
   c. Family meetings are the most cherished meetings of our life .
   d. Family meetings are of the greatest importance in family life.

## Part C

**In this part you'll hear a passage three times. When it is read for the first time, you should listen carefully for its general idea. Then listen to the passage for the second time and fill in the blanks numbered 1 to 7 with the exact words you've just heard. For blanks numbered 8 to 10, fill in the missing information. You can either use the exact words you've just heard or write down the main points in your own words. Finally, check your answers when the passage is read for the third time.** *(10 points)*

It is 1) *estimated* that more than one hundred million Americans eat at least one meal away from home every day. The main reason for this 2) *trend* is that more and more women work and do not have time to cook three meals a day.

There are three categories of dining out in the United States. The first category includes restaurants where people go to 3) *amuse* and 4) *entertain* themselves. In these restaurants 5) *emphasis* is often placed on their 6) *unique* lively atmosphere. Some of them are 7) *decorated* as a saloon of the 19th century American wild west, a village market, or a sailing ship. The second category is to dine out as a special event in special places. 8) *The restaurants in this category can be formal or informal, but they are generally tourist attractions*. The diners do not mind too much about the food. 9) *They just want to have the experience of being there*. The final category of dining out is the convenience restaurants. They include fast-food restaurants such as McDonald's, Kentucky Fried Chicken, Pizza Hut and local ethnic restaurants that offer Chinese, Italian, and Turkish food and so on. 10) *These restaurants open long hours, serve inexpensive food and are conveniently located in neighborhood areas*. They can also be found on highways, at airports and bus terminals.

## Part D

**In this part you'll hear three short passages. Each will be read only once. After each passage, you'll be asked some questions about what was said. Listen carefully and choose the right answer to each question you hear.** *(15 points)*

# Test 2

**Passage 1**

Some people think that they have an answer to the problems of automobile crowding and pollution in large cities. Their answer is the bicycle, or "bike". In a great many cities, hundreds of people ride bicycles to work every day. In New York City, some bike riders have even founded a group called Bike for a Better City. They claim that if more people rode bicycles to work there would be fewer automobiles in the downtown section of the city and therefore less dirty air from car engines.

For several years this group has been trying to get the city government to help bicycle riders. For example, they want the city to paint special lanes — for bicycles only — on some of the main streets, because when bicycle riders must use the same lanes as cars, there may be accidents. Bike for a Better City feels that if there were special lanes, more people would use bikes.

But no bicycle lanes have been painted yet. Not everyone thinks they are a good idea. Taxi drivers don't like the idea — they say it will slow traffic. Some store owners on the main streets don't like the idea — they say that if there is less traffic, they will have less business. And most people live too far from downtown to travel by bike. The city government has not yet decided what to do. It wants to keep everyone happy. On weekends, Central Park — the largest open space in New York — is closed to cars, and the roads may be used by bicycles only. But Bike for a Better City says that this is not enough and keeps fighting to get bicycle lanes downtown. Until that happens, the safest place to bicycle may be in the park.

*Questions 1 to 4 are based on the passage you've just heard.*

1. What is some people's answer to the problems of automobile crowding and pollution?
   a. The truck.
   b. The bus.
   c. The bicycle.
   d. Walking.

2. What is the name of the group recently set up in New York City?
   a. Bike for a Better City.
   b. Bike for a Safer City.
   c. Ride for a Better City.
   d. Ride for a Safer City.

3. What has a bike riders' group been trying to get the city government to do?
   a. Paint additional lanes on the main streets.
   b. Ban the use of cars in Central Park on weekends.
   c. Paint special lanes on some of the main streets for bicycles only.
   d. Restrict traffic on some of the main streets.

4. Which of the following is true according to the passage?
   a. Bike riders in New York City are mostly students.
   b. Bike riders in New York City use the same lanes as cars.
   c. Bike riders in New York City can use special lanes on some of the main streets.
   d. Bike riders in New York City can ride in Central Park without being disturbed by cars.

**Passage 2**

Many nurses at a large hospital report considerable emotional concerns and fears about their work with AIDS patients. In fact, in some situations, well-trained personnel may need to be assigned to special units for AIDS patients, since some nurses might refuse to treat them on a regular basis. In addition, they ask that continuing medical education about AIDS should be provided to hospital staff members.

Responses to a 10-question survey have been obtained from 191 nurses at the hospital, which says that more than 200 AIDS patients have been treated there during the past ten years. One-half of the nurses believed that AIDS could be transmitted to hospital personnel because of contact with patients despite precautions. Furthermore, 85 percent believed that pregnant nurses should not care for AIDS patients, and 39 percent indicated that they would ask for transfer if they had to care for AIDS patients on a regular basis. One-half of the nurses also said they were more frightened caring for AIDS patients than for a patient with a more infectious but less serious disease.

It is not clear if these results apply to all nurses who treat AIDS patients, but the reported emotional concerns are important in light of the increasing number of patients with AIDS seen in general hospitals.

*Questions 5 to 7 are based on the passage you've just heard.*

5. What are nurses in the large hospital complaining about?
   a. The danger of being infected with AIDS.
   b. The pressure of work in the hospital.
   c. The shortage of well-trained health workers for AIDS patients.
   d. The lack of medical education about AIDS for hospital staff.

6. What might some nurses do in this situation?
   a. Ask for special training.
   b. Seek employment in another hospital.
   c. Refuse to be assigned to special units for AIDS patients.
   d. Refuse to treat AIDS patients on a regular basis.

7. What can be inferred from the passage?
   a. Nurses are not afraid of infectious diseases except AIDS.
   b. Something should be done to help deal with the situation of the increasing number of AIDS patients in general hospitals.
   c. Nurses should have a more humanistic attitude towards AIDS patients.
   d. AIDS patients should be treated in special hospitals.

**Passage 3**

American executives sometimes signal their feelings of ease and importance in their offices by putting their feet on the desk while on the telephone. In Japan, people would be shocked. Showing the soles of your feet is the height of bad manners. It is a social insult only exceeded by blowing your nose in public.

The Japanese have perhaps the strictest rules of social and business behavior. Seniority is very important, and a younger man should never be sent to complete a business deal with an older Japanese man. The Japanese business card almost needs a rulebook of its own. You must exchange business cards immediately on meeting because it is essential to establish everyone's status and position.

When it is handed to a person in a superior position, it must be given and received with both hands, and you must take time to read it carefully, and not just put it in your pocket. Also the bow is a very important part of greeting someone. You should not expect the Japanese to shake hands. Bowing the head is a mark of respect and the first bow of the day should be lower than when you meet thereafter. The Americans sometimes find it difficult to accept the more formal Japanese manners. They prefer to be casual and more informal, as illustrated by the universal "Have a nice day!" American waiters have a one-word imperative "Enjoy!" The British, of course, are cool and reserved. The great topic of conversation between strangers in Britain is the weather — unemotional and impersonal. In America, the main topic between strangers is the search to find a geographical link. "Oh, really? You live in Ohio? I had an uncle who once worked there."

*Questions 8 to 10 are based on the passage you've just heard.*

8. Which of the following is considered extremely bad manner by the Japanese?
   a. Putting one's feet on the desk while on the telephone.
   b. Blowing one's nose in public.
   c. Showing the soles of one's feet.
   d. Showing one's feelings of ease and importance in the offices.

9. What do you know about the Japanese in terms of social and business behavior?
   a. They attach great importance to ranks and seniority.

b. They respect the old people very much.

c. They don't allow the young people to complete business deals all by themselves.

d. They think that young people must exchange business cards immediately on meeting old people.

10. What can be learned from the passage?

a. The Japanese never shake hands with others.

b. The Japanese bow often to show their respect to others.

c. The Japanese are more formal than any other people in the world.

d. The Japanese always read business cards carefully before putting them in their pockets.

Total Score: 35 points